Praise for *Ship of Fates*

"Gorgeous prose twines mythology and history in *Ship of Fates*. This fresh, ethereal take on Gold Rush San Francisco and the Chinese-American experience had me mesmerized. I read the entire novella in one sitting."

—Beth Cato, author of *Breath of Earth*

"Legend blends with family lore in this speculative Gold Rush–era tale set amidst the gambling dens and red lanterns of San Francisco's Barbary Coast. Recovering the lost history of nineteenth-century Chinese immigrants, Caitlin Chung spins an uncommon fairy-tale fiction."

—Mia Ayumi Malhotra,
award-winning author of *Isako Isako*

"This gem of a novel is a dazzling, subversive fairy tale, one that both reveals and upends the myth of San Francisco's Barbary Coast. Hints of Calvino and Winterson rise up out of Chung's deft prose, but only as signs that point to a wholly unique voice."

—Lewis Buzbee, author of *The Yellow-Lighted Bookshop*

Ship of Fates

by Caitlin Chung

LANTERNFISH PRESS

PHILADELPHIA

LANTERNFISH PRESS
399 Market Street, Suite 360
Philadelphia, PA 19106
lanternfishpress.com

Cover Design: Kimberly Glyder

Printed in the United States of America.
Library of Congress Control Number: 2019943288
Print ISBN: 978-1-941360-31-6
Digital ISBN: 978-1-941360-32-3

for mom and dad

Ship of Fates

You go to see the Lighthouse Keeper for a story because another story told you to. You've been chasing these stories—the ones about her, about this place, and about the old place, too. It's taken you a while to find her, but you're ready.

It's autumn now. The air is matter-of-fact in its new chill, especially by the bay. You're standing outside the old lighthouse with your hands in your pockets. The wind, unbreakable, pushes against your face. The lighthouse hasn't been in use for a hundred years, but it's been left alone. Nobody goes there. The world has nearly forgotten there's a reason to.

Underneath your arm is a small bundle of kindling you've brought for the Lighthouse Keeper. It's left bits of bark and long splinters stuck to your coat. The lighthouse door, about a foot shorter than you, is crusted with salt and blends into the wall, invisible but for a thin black outline and a brass handle.

You use the side of your fist to bang against the stone. It's a dull thud that you worry won't reach the top. You wait a full minute, listening for sounds inside. The wind feels worse now that you're just waiting. You're right at the edge of the San Francisco Bay, but you feel far, far away from everything; you might as well be the only person left in the world. You bang on the door again and wait.

This time, the door is pushed open, scraping a flattened arc in the dirt at your feet. You bow three times, show you've brought kindling—as the legend directs—and get your first glimpse of her, the Lighthouse Keeper. She holds a candle that illuminates half of her face. Without looking directly at you, she backs away to give you the space to slip inside, wearing an unsurprised sort of expression.

"Hi!" you say, with too much perk. The way she doesn't even acknowledge your greeting tells you not to say any more.

There's a spiral stone staircase. The Lighthouse Keeper begins to climb back up. You assume you are meant to follow. Up, up you trail her—no landings to catch your breath, no banister to lean on, only climbing. The Lighthouse Keeper walks easily, lightly. You, on the other hand, are slowing, panting, burning, and this embarrasses you. You hope she doesn't turn around to find your mouth hanging open and your back slumped. The steps appear to be flecked with gold, more and more densely the higher you go. Her candlelight makes the flecks pop, but only for a second; you're not sure they're actually there. You strain your eyes to look closer.

At the top of the stairs is another door and, beyond it, a perfectly circular room. Inside, gold: every last inch covered in gold. Gold in blocks, nuggets, and dust; stacked, piled, and strewn; it is up the walls halfway to the ceiling. Your feet make prints in the gold dust on the floor. There is a small table with two chairs, and though there are more things, you don't notice them much, not with all the gold around. You feel you must be in the right place.

The Lighthouse Keeper takes the kindling and you stand silent in front of the door while she goes about lighting a fire—now for the chill in her bones, not a sailor's eye searching through the fog, not like when it burned bright and constant each night. She sets a teakettle on the grille. You wonder if you should offer to help, but she moves like you're not there at all. You aren't sure if you should feel like an intruder coming into her lighthouse, or privileged, or scared, or at ease, so you settle for feeling all these things in a cascading sequence, at least until you know which one fits.

She finally sits down on one of the old chintz armchairs that's lost almost all of its upholstery, then lays a woolen blanket over her lap. She gestures for you to sit across from her.

You notice she is not old. You can't figure out why she is called old in rumors and stories; she is barely a woman. You feel a little slighted on her behalf. Her skin is smooth, white as pearl. She has the kind of face that you don't recognize so much as sense to be familiar, if there is such a distinction. In some way, she's family; perhaps that is what you see.

She has noticed you staring but doesn't cower. She is hard to read. She's mysterious in the way wise people are mysterious, knowing so much that they are always involuntarily hiding secrets. You consider that this might be where the rumor of age comes from. It works on her. It works with her eyes—narrow and angled yet slightly wistful in expression—as if she's grown tired of all that knowing. Maybe she is old, after all.

It's as cold inside the tower as out, but at least you're shielded from the wind. You rub your hands together in your lap, trying to warm them. You stare at the fire, which is still catching, and wait for its heat to reach you. You aren't sure what is supposed to happen now, but as soon as you start searching your mind for something to say, she clears her throat. She begins.

1,000 BCE

Once upon a very long time ago, in a country where monsoons bathe the mountaintops, lychee trees flaunt their blushing fruit, and the river runs over a bed of pearls, a girl called Mei became the thief bride. This happened in the village of Huangpu, in the port of Guangzhou: the home of the Wong bloodline.

Her father was a burdened man. Her mother, a tired woman with sunless eyes. Her sisters were collapsed promises for brothers, small and plain and penitent. This was Mei's family.

Mei was the eldest, both rich with her yet unclaimed beauty and menaced by it. She dreamed of being free, of catching fever at the hearth of the wide world's commons. Which is to say, she wanted to find love.

What is more commonplace than love?

What is more trite than wanting love when you're destined down the river?

Her father promised her hand to a man who spoke a strange tongue. The man had come by trade ship from a faraway land. He came with his salt-licked sailors to lay claim to the treasures of Guangzhou's spring. And along with them, to Mei, for an amount of gold as dense and deep as need. She was fourteen.

It was a moonless night when Mei stole her suitor's gold. She ran away from home, a whole violent ocean away. The gold was carried in the belly of a whale that swam for seven days and seven nights while Mei rode on its back. When they came to this coast with its welcoming bay, she threw the gold into the rivers of this land to be forever lost in the creases of poppy-covered hills. The gold was gone, spread where no gold was before, nor was ever meant to be.

The Wong family was disgraced. Mei's hand was bereft of its promise. But still she bears a debt: She cannot rest until she gives back what she took. Here in this lighthouse she is cursed to stay until she recovers all the gold; here she must light the fires that draw greed to her doorstep. Here, by magic, the fires stay lit each night, a mirror for the feral hope of her search—so long as she continues to try and find every nugget. Here Wong Zhi Mei, the maker of Gold Mountain, remains.

The Lighthouse Keeper tells this story like one she's memorized
from a book; she pretends she isn't a part of it. You've heard the
story before. Everybody has. It's the story that explains why
there is so much gold in California, where there'd never been gold
before, where there was never meant to be any. It's the story that's
been repeated in teahouses, in mahjong parlors, in children's pic-
ture books, and by the mouths of grandmothers for thousands of
years. What you hope will follow, however, has only been told to
those who know there is more story that follows, and who go in
search of it.

She is silent, and it occurs to you that nothing might follow.
Perhaps this is all she thinks you came for. Perhaps there really
isn't more to the story. You look for hints in the way she sits. You
aren't even warmed yet. The fire has barely started; the kindling
you brought is still alight. She can't be done.

This story she's told, "Maker of Gold Mountain," is so familiar
that it's been a long time since you paid attention. The words are

the same, but until now, you feel like you've never really listened. You know it as the story of what brought your ancestors here, and of how all the gold came to be in California. But this time, you hear it like a secret.

This is when the Lighthouse Keeper's teakettle whistles like a Transamerica train. There is something aged in the way she lifts herself from her chair and shuffles through the gold dust on the floor. She is slow to pull the kettle from the heat, and the whistle blares—uncomfortably long, uncomfortably loud. You look around like it might have disturbed someone nearby. The Lighthouse Keeper pours two cups of tea. She lets them steep, does not carry them back to where you sit, waits for a deep brew. She stares into the growing fire, restless, as if she were rousing things from darker places than memory. You suspect the fire hasn't lit itself in many years, not since she gave up on breaking her curse, and you wonder how the warmth, the light of it might make her feel. Minutes pass.

You feel nervous when the Lighthouse Keeper hands you a cup of tea and retakes her seat. The tea smells like trees. It's too hot to sip but you keep it in your cold hands, already feeling better. The Lighthouse Keeper adjusts the blanket in her lap. She, too, keeps the tea in her hands. For the first time all night, she looks you straight in the eye. You are so intimidated that you can't even begin to parse her expression. And then she looks away, past you, over your shoulder, like she's staring at a distant horizon.

There was once a girl whose name was etched into the water so that she might never feel lost. Hold a seashell to her ear and she will tell you what it sounds like when the world is leaking. She shook the clotted language from her mouth and found that her teeth were brass, chipped and broken by the edges of destiny, then replaced with pearls.

Fate is made of water, made to fit itself into the last spaces left open in a life. Made to be needed. Drop a stone into still water and watch the way the ripples wrinkle and never break. Count the rings before they stop. Maybe then.

You feel unprepared for this. You wonder if everything from now on will be so cryptic, because you have absolutely no idea what she means. The sequence of possible feelings cascades over you again. You realize you have not said another word to the Lighthouse Keeper, but you sense this isn't the time to start. She has paused only for a second to sip her tea, so you wait.

The Lighthouse Keeper holds her teacup in both hands and takes short sips. You can tell she's ignoring the fact that it's still too hot.

You feel warmth from the fire now, and the autumn chill is leaving your clothes and skin. Your hands are relaxed around the teacup and you also take a tentative sip. It is so bitter you struggle to keep from grimacing. It tastes like a forest full of age and deep earth and dampness. But once the taste fades, you realize it has filled you with energetic heat. It appears to have done the same for her. The next part she tells has a different tone, as if she might fool you into thinking it's not still her story.

1849

It began with a ship, its figurehead a mermaid wearing nothing but a flowered crown, her tits to the sun. The ship sailed into the San Francisco Bay's harbor with the great and uncontrollable urgency of a young man losing his virginity. It coasted straight onto the thick sandbar until it dragged to a halt and stuck in place—the bow up on dry beach, the stern in the shallows where the water lapped at its sides. A short way back from the harbor rose a steep cliff, and from the top a stone lighthouse dropped its shadow over the deck of the ship, a shadow shaped unambiguously like an erect dick.

The discovery of gold in California was news that had crossed oceans and continents. You can pluck nuggets right off the ground, they said. You can scrape the bottom of your boot for enough dust to buy yourself a fine night with a fine woman. In California, they said, luck is as common as riches are plentiful. Go, and you will find your fortune. The stories pulled like a Pacific current.

The captain and his crew had come from the other side of the world, their curly hair as thick as the brogue in their mouths, their skin as fair as their manners were not. They came impatiently. They had told their mothers and their wives, their farmhands and herders: "We're going to see the elephant! We're going to strike gold!" They were certain that the elephant, magnificent and conspicuous, would be waiting.

The journey here had been long. It had been a lurching ramble. A rocking, swaying ship; a drunk mother's cradle. The sailors were beaten by the wind, by the sun glaring overhead and glancing off isles of ice. Days passed when it didn't seem they traversed a single mile—days of empty blue on blue, when it was easy to forget if anything else had ever existed. They'd grown beastlier with each new face of the moon, their hair and beards tangled, their temperaments barbed, lips curled over teeth. How quickly hope turns itself savage and starved.

When the California coastline finally appeared in the spyglass like a smudge at the bottom of the lens, the ship picked up speed. The sailors measured the closing miles by their growing feverishness. They never considered collapsing the sails nor dropping the anchor as the ship barreled into port. The bow bobbed as the hull scraped over large rocks underwater. The sound of wood raking over sand and gravel echoed within the basin of the bay. The sailors on board seemed not to mind the tumult, and when the ship finally ground to a stop, almost fully on the beach, and the wood, which had been screeching under the strain, quieted, the captain and his crew disembarked. They waddled away in their bloated boots like ducklings. They abandoned the ship, eager to find their fortunes, and were never seen again.

All except for one lonely sailor. He watched the last of his fellows set off across the beach, out of the lighthouse's shadow and into the sun. He took in the thin fog, the way it smelled like the tide, and he felt at home. Out at sea, there are no smells—not of the human world, not of reassurance. For the first time in many months, he could think in other colors besides blue. He was relieved for the stillness of the beached ship. He was relieved to be away from men without women. The sailor limped to the helm of the ship, favoring his sore foot. He'd never been at the helm, never set his palms on the wheel, but he gripped it now like a ladder rung and surveyed the land.

This was San Francisco, a city stained yellow—yellow in the flowers and gold in the waters. This was the city by the bay, shrouded in fog that came in off the Pacific and reluctantly withdrew in the morning. To the south, the bay opened and fanned out like a hand of cards. In the north, the coastline was one long stretch of cliff, perfectly vertical and domineering, as if a knife had come tearing down for a slice of sea-salted earth. At the top of the cliff, there was the lighthouse.

The lonely sailor, a man of few words and fewer aspirations, lifted his hand over his brow to see beyond the lighthouse's shadow and onto the waterfront street.

The people of his homeland had told stories of America and its men, who shouldered the starry burden of opportunity like a knapsack heavy with fate. Wherever a story could be told, it was about California and its golden mystique. But he did not see the allure. He did not see much of anything but delusion and an arrogant army of miners running inland, their pockets weighted only with possibility. He was sensible. He stayed in the deserted port.

His name was Jack.

Back home, Jack was a man known to have a quick draw and a sure shot, and he made a lot of money off that quick draw and sure shot, as well as off any other wager he could afford. He got by until, like they do, his reputation eclipsed him, and nobody would bet against him anymore. Then he stopped getting by.

He had never cherished dreams of California gold but rather had boarded the ship because all the potatoes in his father's farmland had been dug up and boiled. The depths of hunger tunneled endlessly still. He'd been too much a burden, a man of no trade but a practiced gunshot grown bankrupt of use. When he kissed his ma goodbye, he took nothing but the clothes on his back, his favorite revolver, and a gold tooth inside his left cheek. Then he let the ship carry him an ocean away as the sailors' songs of gold lulled him to sleep each night.

Above him, the sails ballooned and flapped, drawing on the riggings with strained whines. The masts creaked. The ropes slapped against the poles. The wind was trying to keep the ship moving, insistent for the journey to continue. The ship was a woman arguing with herself, one half pushing forward, the other digging in her heels.

Jack limped from the helm to the deck and set about taking the sails down. He thought of the countless times he'd pulled on these ropes with his whole body's weight, keeping them taut and the ship on course. They'd passed through storms and high winds, and he had always been the one to tame her, to convince her he knew best. And now he was undressing the ship, unclipping her garters and letting the cloth fall. It was difficult work alone and with a bum foot, and he went about it slowly and sensually. He was absorbed with her, the way a man is when what he needs is a real woman. She was his alone, and he belonged to her just the same.

In the days and nights that followed, Jack did little but sit up in the crow's nest, where the sky surrounded him and the air smelled sweet. The ship was oak wood, chewed up and rough from the long journey here. During the day, the phallic shadow of the lighthouse kept her in perpetual shade. At night she was fitfully lit by the lighthouse's fire, where shadows played and hid. The stern of the ship remained swollen and smooth, darkened by the puddled bay water that lapped at the sides. The masts were splintered and brittle, but the crow's nest was strangely unweathered. He sat with his ankles up on the railing, hoping the fresh air might help heal his foot.

On the way here to San Francisco, nobody had known him or his prowess with a gun, and he'd won himself a little money. He'd made a bet with a stub-nosed kid called Patrick Christopher Michael O'Leary Laughlin, whose name was longer than his stamina. Patrick Christopher Michael O'Leary Laughlin was generally a little shit, but they had one thing in common: They were easily wooed by a gamble, pulled into that frivolous romance only to confuse it for love; nothing was as important as the chance to win. This was why Patrick Christopher Michael O'Leary Laughlin bet he could outshoot Jack, and why Jack accepted the challenge.

They placed two whiskey bottles on the deck railing, one for each of them; shoot on three. If they both broke their bottles, the fastest man won. But when they holstered their guns for the count, Patrick Christopher Michael O'Leary Laughlin accidentally shot Jack's little toe clean off.

It was somewhat healed now, but Jack's balance would never come back. His shot was vaguely bent, off by just enough that he hadn't won another bet with his revolver since. It was as if everything—his shot, his luck, his livelihood—had all been kept in that little toe, now blown off his foot like a barnacle from the underbelly. He'd struggled to complete the journey with only one good foot. Most of the other sailors felt bad for him, but not enough to say so. Gambling men don't tend to get anything but the bad kind of pity.

Jack left the bottles there on the railing, and whenever one fell, he replaced it. He'd taken many more shots at them, but all of his bullets were fed to the sea. Now he'd given up trying his shot, but he kept a row of bottles there nonetheless. He eyed them from his seat in the crow's nest. He held his revolver, unloaded, to his eye and aimed at one of the bottles. He kept his sight over the barrel and scanned the entire San Francisco Bay. He liked to point his gun when he observed the world around him. He could focus, see the details. He could breathe steady, tongue pressed to his gold tooth, and let the sight on his revolver steer his one-eyed gaze. It was peaceful, and he was happy watching the days pass with nothing but the lazy flight of gulls to mark the time.

Before long, the San Francisco Bay teemed with ships. Some unloaded passengers and left again. Some stayed, just like Jack's, anchoring all around like canvas-winged bugs desperate for the lighthouse fire, and together they became the Barbary Coast.

The Barbary Coast sprang from the shrugs that said, *What now?* It developed out of necessity, out of there being a city's worth of people and no city. And like most things born of necessity, the Barbary Coast was all instinct and no insight. It was the place for drinks, a bride at any price, or a red-lamp romp, where well-juiced judgments played out by moonlight. It was a city of fools—fools arriving to pass on through to the Gold Rush, fools who'd already blown it at the Gold Rush and come back, and people who saw all these fools as the opportunities they were. Like Jack.

Jack started by moving all of the ship's furniture into the main cabin and making as much use of it as he could—crates for a bar, barrels for stools, rowboats for seats. He packed the main cabin full, leaving aisles barely wide enough to slip through. He hung sails over the portholes and windows to dampen any light from outside. He kept exactly one poker table—his table—where he could still scratch that gambling itch good and long. Then he traded his gold tooth for a watered-down barrel of whiskey and waited for the crowds he knew would find him. When they did, reckless and indecent, he sold them whiskey until he could also buy ale, then sold whiskey and ale until he could buy gin, and then food, and so on, until his ship became the Barbary Coast's first public house and he needed to hire some help.

First, he hired an overbearing and devout woman, Dolores, to cook, because there is no home without a good Catholic woman with good Catholic sense to help run it. Dolores was nearly deaf in one ear and the other wasn't much use either. She spoke close, loud, and moist. She liked to share gossip dressed as the Good Word. She kept her hair back with a rag kerchief and had a fuzzy chin, and once hired she could always be found in the kitchen, a large mixing bowl pinned against her hipbone, waving a wooden spoon like a ruling scepter while delivering her stories like sermons.

Jack immediately liked Dolores, her prying air and plump body and the way she *tut-tutted* her disapproval of his gun. Dolores disapproved of the Gold Rush, too, and certainly of the Barbary Coast; it was too much of a middle finger to manners. But she thoroughly enjoyed disapproving of things, so she stayed. She believed that gold would only reveal itself to the people of God and that anyone else who came to find it was sure to meet a horrible end. She believed that to cook for someone was to be the instrument of God's will, which just about made her a saint, and she believed the fact that she cooked for the scum of the earth was irrelevant. Dolores piously and uncomplicatedly believed, and she worked hard.

She cooked and cleaned in the kitchen until nearly dawn, when she could go down and get some sleep in the bedroom Jack had made for her in the belly of the ship. She talked all the time in her low, muttering way—to God, to herself, to anyone who passed by the kitchen window—and when the night's revelry dragged on into the lightening of the sky, she came into the bar to lecture the remaining drunks. Her rebukes slipped through the seams of scripture and materialized as pure, old-fashioned guilt. When she was done lecturing, she held them to her breast while they cried about their lives.

Dolores was happy enough on Jack's ship until Mei came knocking. She had never seen a Chinese person before—she would never associate with the kind of person who would even think about associating with an Oriental, heaven forbid. She'd only seen pictures in the newspaper, so she expected someone who looked like a serpentine monster with its skin stretched too tightly around its skull. With claws and bigger teeth. She was surprised by Mei's slight and prim softness in voice and body. Mei disappointed Dolores. A real-life Chinese person was not much to talk about.

Mei came to Jack's ship looking for work. She kept from them the fact that she was the lighthouse keeper, knowing the rumors of magic. She kept from them any glimpse of who she was. She'd been watching the ship, listening, since the day Jack took the sails down. She'd seen him move furniture around and drag barrels of liquor up onto the deck. She'd heard the nighttime crowds get thicker and stay later, and she'd heard the drunken lamentations of those who sat across from Jack at his poker table, which gave her an idea.

Early one morning, Mei went over to the ship carrying a gift of egg custards for breakfast—the first offense against Dolores, who was a jealous cook—and told Jack she would like a job as his poker dealer. He immediately liked the idea; of course he wanted a house dealer. But among all the contradictory things said about the Chinese, there was a resounding opinion that they were untrustworthy. What would be said of keeping an Oriental in his bar? Would people stop coming? He studied Mei's face. She had the kind of face that pleasantly hid whatever she was thinking. She hadn't spoken another word. Jack had heard that Oriental women were good that way. He handed her a deck of cards and was pleased to see them relax into her hands like warm sand. She was good that way, too, and without any more thought he offered her a whiskey a night to be the dealer.

Jack explained to Mei that if a man wanted to play, he played; the table was never closed. And if a man wanted to play, he put down a .45mm bullet as his ante.

Even at the poker table, Jack's gun never left his hand. He liked everyone to know that he'd put a bullet—*their* bullet—right between the eyes of a cheater. He took any bet, would play for anything if it was placed on the table. Sometimes it was money; sometimes it was other riches; sometimes it was shoelaces. It didn't matter—he played.

Dolores and Mei never warmed to each other. Each night they eyed one another across the room, put off by the smug expression they saw on each other's faces. Dolores thought Mei was untrustworthy, like any other Chinese, and she'd heard plenty about how untrustworthy the Chinese were. She thought there was something a little disturbing about Mei; where did she get off acting like she *wasn't* Chinese? Mei was too much at ease; she had to be hiding something.

Jack noticed none of this. He was making money and drinking and gambling. He was the kind of unhappy that is easily confused with contentment, and in this way, with his ship the pioneer of the Barbary Coast, he carried on.

You think about the feeling of not knowing what to expect yet
being surprised by it, which you deem to be a deceptive feeling.
There's a new edge to the Lighthouse Keeper—a sailor's slant to
her wisdom, a willfulness in how she says shit *and* tits *and* dick.
She's easy to listen to, her voice like bedtime comfort. She doesn't
tell this story in the same rehearsed way she told the first. You can
see her remembering as the words form in her mouth. There's a
cadence that admits, yes, this is her story.

The fact that the story is set in a specific era throws you off. You
hadn't expected it to belong to time. The story of how all the gold
got to California is a world away from the one where it all gets
dug up. You feel disoriented and look out the window, half expect-
ing to see the beached ships still out there. Seeing nothing but
darkness, you wonder how you could possibly be in San Francisco
without so much as a light or echo of them.

The Lighthouse Keeper has been watching you. You must have looked as though you needed a break. She is more relaxed now than she was. She sips her tea and keeps a pleasant, almost imperceptible smile on her face. It's a smile of memory. You smile back at her, though it feels strange. It feels like you've mistaken something, like her smile was not for you and by smiling back you've stolen it from her. She takes another sip of tea. Then her eyes go back to that horizon somewhere over your shoulder and she continues.

🚢

A few months passed. It was an unusually warm night in autumn when Patrick Christopher Michael O'Leary Laughlin, the man who'd shot off Jack's little toe, appeared in his pub. Patrick had found nothing and lost everything else in the Gold Rush. He'd come back to the Barbary Coast for the soup lines and to look for work. With some panhandled coins, he'd patched up a shipwrecked rowboat he found half buried on the beach. He started fishing and then selling his catches.

Patrick was nearly done with his first drink when he finished telling Jack his story. He held his glass in a way that said he was unsure yet hopeful it would be filled again. Like a poor man. He looked older, brittle like a homesick starfish, though not half a year had passed since he and Jack had arrived in San Francisco. On the journey over, he'd been filled with the relentless conviction that he'd strike it rich, but his expression was now sloped in a manner that betrayed self-loathing disappointment. There was more space between his words, and that space was full of sadness. Jack liked him better this way—a man who'd lost everything and then went and got some back.

Earlier that afternoon, Patrick had sold Dolores a handsome trout, which was how he came to sit at Jack's bar. Jack bought Patrick more drinks, and Patrick apologized again and again for Jack's lost toe. This went on for hours—it was so nice to see someone from the homeland. This was why they were so very drunk and singing folk songs when Madam Toy came in, and why they never noticed the Chinaman, or his bride, at all.

Madam Toy, the Chinaman, and his bride came in together and stood by the bar. The patrons of Jack's ship were unaccustomed to giving a shit, so, contrary to the Chinaman's worries, they weren't bothered. It was Dolores, who'd taken over pouring drinks while Jack and Patrick drank themselves cockeyed, who was bothered. She still hadn't fully gotten over Mei's presence or the idea of the Chinese in general. She poured whiskey and watched closely and made her judgments. Dolores was the only one who saw Madam Toy scan the room and catch Mei's eye at the poker table. Mei was sitting there, alone and anxious, and upon seeing Madam Toy she sat up a little straighter, then idly brought the deck of cards into her hands to shuffle.

The Chinaman and his bride barely looked at one another. Their bodies were angled elsewhere and they kept their eyes low. It was not a good idea for the Chinese to look around too much.

The Chinaman looked like he was just a kid, too young for work to wear on his hands or face, and he didn't know how to hide his nerves. His name was Wayne. Actually, his name was Huang. Huang Jin Bo. He and his bride came from China, from Guangzhou, on a boat, and all the way he'd practiced saying in English: My name is Huang Jin Bo. He'd said it perfectly. But the man at the pier wrote down in his book, *Wayne Jimbo*. Now that was his name. That's how things were for the Chinese.

His bride was called Annie, but there wasn't any story to it. Annie, above anything else, was pissed off. The drink in her hand, her first ever, was spreading heat and defiance from her stomach out, and she was feeling like she didn't give any fucks about anything.

She had long, long hair that fell into her lap, and she wound it around one of her fingers the way someone might play with a knife while threatening someone else. In her other hand she held on to a pendant of a lotus flower that hung from her neck on a gold chain. Her father had given it to her as a sort of apologetic farewell when he pushed her onto the boat with Wayne for no reason but having an auspicious eleventh toe. Leave it to batty old village women to spread rumors that an eleventh toe was lucky. She'd never even met Wayne before the day they embarked. She wore a white dress with a square collar that came down to her small calves, and her ankles were crossed and tucked beneath her. She was beautiful in a way that seemed stolen from another creature, soft and girlish, but her rage was all woman.

Annie couldn't decide whom she disliked more— Wayne or Madam Toy. Madam Toy had appeared as soon as they'd stepped off the boat in San Francisco's harbor, as if she were expecting them. The man they knew as Mr. Zhou, the one who had fixed their tickets to America, brought them over to her. Mr. Zhou was flamboyant and smarmy, aggressive in his vanity, in his oiled black hair and stoutness. He was the kind of man who stuck his fork in your plate for a taste of your dinner, the unannounced and well-fed scavenger, the kind of man who put *Mr.* before his name to sound more American. He was too interested in them. In her. Too careful making sure he knew their details. But once aboard, he did not so much as look at them. Next they saw of him, he was introducing Madam Toy as their auntie there on the landing dock, and then he disappeared.

Madam Toy also came from the same village in Guangzhou; she was of the same Wong bloodline if you went far back enough, and so they were family. Madam Toy convinced Wayne to come with her onto Jack's ship, explaining that Chinese were allowed at his poker table and it had white-man value. Wayne was embarrassed he didn't have anything with which to start their lives here. It had cost everything just to get onto the boat from China. He felt the responsibility of a husband but none of the affection, which left him willing to trust anyone who promised him a dollar.

When Wayne saw that the dealer was Chinese, he felt more comfortable being there. But when Annie saw that the dealer was Chinese, she became more nervous. If they won, they would be accused of cheating. How could Wayne fail to realize this? Madam Toy was walking them into a trap, prodding Wayne toward the poker table and gesturing for Annie to sit at the bar and act invisible.

Once Madam Toy and Wayne sat across from Mei, Jack and Patrick came and sat too. Jack didn't leave anyone sitting there without him for very long. He took any and every bet laid on the table, and he did it right away. He'd seen Madam Toy once or twice before. She had an intrusive face, contradictory to her beauty. It was a youthful beauty, though there was something old about the way she possessed it. It was rumored that Madam

Toy was one of the only Chinese women around, and the only one worth undressing. It was also rumored that she was an unforgiving gambler. They said she'd once sliced a man's testicles off with a kitchen knife and kept them in a jar. They said taking his testicles for no reason other than a wager was the only thing she would go down to her knees for. She didn't pray, either.

Fresh whiskey was poured in fresh glasses, and Jack, Patrick, Madam Toy, and Wayne played their first few rounds to little consequence. The cards were dealt and collected, dealt and collected. Mei's hands were fluid and the cards were a part of them. Her presence was like water. She hadn't said a word all night, hadn't so much as looked at anyone too long, not since she first met Madam Toy's eye. Again she collected, shuffled, and dealt the cards, and a hand came that would change everything.

The bar had emptied except for Annie—and Dolores, who was practically breathing in Annie's face, so unwilling was she to take her eyes off the bizarre situation of four Chinese together in one place—which, even more bizarrely, was the place she was also in. The room had become calm in a peculiar way, and a silence most often reserved for high mass came down upon them. A few rounds of betting passed and a small mountain of treasures collected in the center of the table. Nobody was ready to fold. The room was lit by candles, now dripping low, which gave a wild, insecure feeling, as if they might go out and erase everything into darkness. Everyone shifted their weight on the peg-legged stools. Everyone's faces were twisted in deliberation.

Madam Toy was next to put a bet on the table, and she didn't care to sit here much longer. She'd tired of the trinkets and the coins; couldn't they get on with it already? She knew what she wanted.

"I'll offer a night between my legs."

She sat back from the table like she knew exactly how long it had been since any of them had seen a girl naked.

Patrick toyed with a ring he wore on his pinky—a claddagh with a yellow heart stone that rested like an egg in the hairs of his knuckle. He had wide, swollen hands puckered from water, knuckles like cherries. He wiggled the ring up and over his knuckle and then pushed it back down into its nest. He let his mind spin stakes from straw, the way it will when everything you have has not yet arrived from the future.

"Fish," was what he said. He wouldn't fold. "I bet fish, a lifetime of fish. I'll deliver it every week."

"Oysters," Madam Toy said, because Patrick and his bet were so pathetic, why not make it harder? Then Madam Toy and Patrick engaged in a slow-burning stare, which Madam Toy knew to be business, which Patrick mistook for flirting, and which made the rest of the table feel awkward.

"Oysters," said Patrick, smiling and forgetting that anyone else was in the room. When the stare moved on to Wayne, who was next to bet, Patrick couldn't help feeling derailed.

Wayne had one thought: *How did I get here?* He could remember his father bringing Mr. Zhou around—Mr. Zhou, well known throughout the village for smuggling teas and silks and relatives, the one who decided who got on a boat and who didn't. Wayne could remember the handshakes and being too afraid to ask what it was his father had done for the tickets. He could remember the ceaseless rocking of the ocean, but everything else spun too quickly in his mind to catch. His eyes were blown out of focus; they were seeing too much at once. The pile of wagers on the table would set him up for long enough to find work, and he wanted it so badly the want had turned to insistent belief he'd win it. But he didn't have anything that would come close to calling the previous bets; he'd already taken the only piece of jewelry—the necklace— from Annie. He didn't have anything else to keep himself in the game.

"I bet," he started, speaking slowly in his heavy accent, then trailed off into a long pause. He'd hoped that if he just started speaking the rest would reveal itself. After an excruciating moment, during which he studied his cards as if they would turn into a reasonable bet, it did.

"The girl," Madam Toy said.

Annie. He didn't know Annie. He hadn't known her before she'd become Annie, either. He knew her face, which family she belonged to, and that her father was willing to double a dowry for her to come here with him, the dowry that had dried up on the journey alone. But he did not know her, and Madam Toy was right in assuming that she was the only possession he had left to wager.

He would win. He felt it. And if he didn't, maybe it would be good for her to go with someone else. He wasn't capable of keeping a wife. She would have a better life without him. He felt that too. This was an opportunity for her, and giving her an opportunity like this was a kindness. Besides, where was the honor in folding now? All of these things made it easy to agree.

"Okay, the girl," he said, and the look on Madam Toy's face made him feel proud. Next he looked over at Annie watching him and felt defensive. He was doing this for them. For her. He would walk away a winner and she would be taken care of. Or he would walk away a loser and she would be taken care of. How was she failing to realize this? She looked at him with such elegant ire that he knew her expression would never leave his memory. He knew without her saying anything what she was thinking, and he wanted to tell her she was wrong to be thinking it.

She was thinking that she did not give one shit about Wayne Jimbo and, though she didn't smoke, she'd rather like a cigarette, because that seemed like the right thing to have in a moment like this one. She was becoming more pissed off by the second, because this was her life. Every time she thought it, *this is my life*, she tipped more liquor past her lips. Wayne had wanted to come to this pub to make enough money to do something besides starve, and here he was being just another small and desperate Chinaman. The feeling of the whiskey glass in her hand and of sitting on a stool that brought her up to look down made her feel powerful, as a salty swell of wrath will do, powerful enough to tell that Wayne Jimbo and that bitch Madam Toy to go right ahead and fuck themselves.

Annie finished off the whiskey in her glass. She imagined slipping out into the night and making it on her own. But she knew she wouldn't. She had nothing. She would have to find another desperate Chinaman to take her in, and that would be no better. Or she would have to find a white man to take her in, and it might as well be one of the drunk ones at the table with Wayne. She kind of liked the one with the limp, anyway. He looked gentle and sedate, easy in a way she hadn't seen or felt since leaving Guangzhou.

Jack was also looking Annie over. Angry women had a way of putting a little wind in his sails. He thought that he would like very much to see her naked. He was not interested in any of the other things put on the table— the oysters, Madam Toy's company, miscellaneous trinkets—but his interest in Annie was rapidly taking control of him. He most likely would never have noticed her had she not been wagered; he did not pay much attention to his own patrons. But now she was on the poker table; there was nothing he'd ever pursued that wasn't presented in the center of a poker table, and there had been nothing as valuable as her in the center of a poker table that he didn't pursue.

He pressed his tongue to where his gold tooth had once been, back before he started his pub. He took his trusty revolver from his hip and spun the chamber with a flick of his middle fingertip. He had no idea what to do next except keep scratching that gambling itch. He had to put a considerable wager down. He had to prove to Annie that he wanted her, had to risk a matching value to make her happy. He wanted to be the one to make her happy, because that's what wanting to see someone naked will do. It was this and self-pity for his lost toe that spurred him along.

"I bet this ship," he said. What else did he have?

"Your kitchen hand, too," Madam Toy said.

Jack didn't argue—men don't argue with women like Madam Toy—but a sharp gasp came from Dolores behind the bar, followed by her flailing to cross herself. Jack refused to look her way; he knew if he did he would crumble under the guilt. He hadn't been thinking of her at all and so betrayed her. The whole table fell dumb. The men at the table were quickly buckling under their bravado, their faces giving away the fact that they were all nauseous and sad. The last seconds before the players revealed their hands were the last seconds any of them would remember as belonging to a simpler time.

Because of course Madam Toy won, which was what they all thought, Annie and Dolores most of all, when she did.

Madam Toy leaned over to collect the coins and trinkets from the table, fingering and appraising each one with exaggerated movements. She crammed them into her bra one by one, each time lifting her eyes to the player who'd lost that item. A final and glancing *fuck you*. She wished she could put their pride in there too and prop her tits to her chin, but she settled with just knowing they'd lost it. She was a real bitch, and she loved it. It didn't matter that the entire night had been set up from the start. She met Mei's eye for only a second as she continued collecting her winnings, relieved that the game was over and forgetting, momentarily, the fact that it had only just begun.

Jack, Patrick, and Wayne blinked away the trance of the last hand. Their legs were stiff, their mouths dry, and while the world unfroze, an uninvited cloud of hindsight ballooned above them. Jack spun the chamber of his gun and it whirred with small clicks. He spun it again, many times, as if it might rewind the night. Until Madam Toy snatched it from him and the cylinder stopped. The table was startled by the quick grab and the tension that followed. Jack was embarrassed, but he would not try to grab his toy back like a child.

"From pity, I will offer you an out," Madam Toy said. She took a .45mm bullet that had been left on the table for the ante and dropped it into the chamber. She spun it and it clicked into place. "One shot to the temple. If you live, I will give you back your wager." She put the gun back in Jack's hands. "You first."

Jack rotated the gun in the light. His big hands tumbled over it. He'd had it forever, since it was pawned by a pirate, or so the shopkeeper had said. There were nicks and scratches on the barrel and blackened hinges where the cylinder snapped in and out of place. Now his own gun felt odd in his hand, like someone else's hold had worn into the wooden grip. It was heavier, the smell of metal and soot too sour. The first thing he'd ever shot was a stray tomcat sleeping on his ma's mailbox. He had fired the shot through the slats of his front porch and clipped its ear. What he remembered most was the way the cat stopped to glare at him before running away. It was the look Dolores had now standing behind the bar. He wanted to say he was sorry but knew that it would make things worse. He wanted to tell her he would take it up with God for her and everything would work out. He wanted to tell Annie he was sorry, too, but couldn't explain what for.

Meanwhile, Madam Toy fielded similar glares from Mei for risking her plan. There was no purpose to the risk and it could cost Mei her life. Mei's hands became sweaty holding the deck of cards. Her heart beat fast as she studied Jack studying his gun and prayed he wouldn't match Madam Toy's stupidity. She was so close, but Madam Toy attempting to one-up her own egotistical malice could set her back to the beginning. Again.

"Keep it all," Jack said, his voice dragging like sand-scuffed footsteps. Mei exhaled deep relief.

Jack, however, felt bad, because bad is the only way to feel when you've lost everything. It was the only time he'd ever turned down a wager. He started to hand the gun off to the next player, but Patrick and Wayne both pushed away from the table with their hands up. Jack emptied the chamber into his palm and put the bullet in his pocket. Madam Toy walked to the bar where Annie sat. She said something softly in Chinese, tucked a stray hair behind Annie's ear, and patted her cheek.

"I am Madam Toy," she said to Dolores as if answering a question. Then she poured herself a drink and went below deck to examine her new ship.

Meanwhile, Jack snuck out of the barroom. He didn't want to get caught talking with Patrick, who'd taken an entire bottle of liquor and was nursing it like a child while whining about oysters. The ship belonged to Madam Toy now, but Jack wanted to sit up in the crow's nest one more time. He climbed up.

The crow's nest was a wide circle with oak railings and slatted walls. The topmast came straight up through the center of the floor and extended into the sky. Jack could see in every direction for miles. He could see the entire bay and the Barbary Coast sprawled at its edge. The bobbing gaslights in the packed harbor created an idyllic scene; he looked down on the deck of his ship, trying to absorb the fact it was no longer his. He felt the kind of disbelief that makes you laugh too easily and sweat. Like waking from a dream you're both disappointed and relieved to exit.

He took off his shoes and socks. He rested against the

topmast and propped his ankles up on the railing, feeling the cool air on his feet. He thought about how things might have been different if he still had his little toe but found it hard to imagine. The concept of possibility was expired and unreachable. Sitting there in the crow's nest, he was high enough to look straight through the open lighthouse window and into the burning fire. He closed his eyes against the orange light and toyed with his gun.

Annie had followed Jack out of the barroom. She had watched him climb up and sit and fiddle with his gun. She liked the way his hands were restless. She liked his few words and his tallness. She liked that whenever he looked over at her, he seemed more awake. Liking these things was what made her decide to climb up and sit beside him in the crow's nest. Without speaking she settled onto the floor, leaned back against the topmast, and stretched her legs out in front of her. She quickly found that next to Jack was a nice place to sit. She liked his comfortable moodiness. She liked being high up in the air. There was no wind. The bay was perfectly flat and metallic, and both of them, for the first time since arriving in San Francisco, felt peaceful. She noticed that he'd rolled up the sleeves of his shirt since the poker game. She noticed that he'd removed his shoes and socks. Then she spotted his missing toe, let out a sort of squeal that made Jack jump, and ripped off her own left shoe.

There, next to her pinky, was the extra toe. She wiggled it, waiting for him to see it. Annie's family believed that eleventh toe made her lucky. It meant she was the girl in the family sent to America, for an extra toe was an extra root to put down in American soil. She had been so angry about her toe, angry with her father for giving her away because of it and then angry for being given away again by Wayne. But suddenly that eleventh toe felt lucky.

When Jack saw her extra pinky toe, he swore he felt his missing one come back into its place. The sense of completeness made him want to touch her. Annie felt it too, that kind of completeness that is whimsical and optimistic, as if to say this can't be anything but destiny. Destiny, when it appears through the shade of defeat, can really turn you on.

Annie let this idea of destiny envelop them, let it mingle with her drunken anger. And because nothing soothes an enraged heart like climbing onto a stranger's lap, and nothing sells a bad decision like thinking it's destined, she kissed him. She brought his face into her neck and let him run his big, restless hands up her dress. She was taken aback by Jack's otherness. She touched the freckles all over his arms, touched his rough beard, noticed his light eyes were like water under a foggy sky. She reached for his belt and he pulled his pants down. She wanted to lose her virginity and cancel out her value. She suspected things might end up better for her if she did. She could stop being a pawn to everyone else, and maybe then she could even go with Jack instead of Madam Toy. She hiked up her skirt and lowered herself onto him, then bit her lip when he sharply ripped through her. She didn't really know what to do after that, so she let him grip her waist and move her up and down on top of him until he finished. The sex was short and self-righteous and left them both feeling like they'd accomplished something important. Afterward, he held her.

A soft wind came, and Jack and Annie listened to it moving through the masts, which creaked ever so slightly, until the sound of Madam Toy crossing the deck into the barroom and back out punctured the quiet. She had been hastily memorizing the layout of the ship. She hadn't seen Jack or Annie in a while, though at first she didn't notice. Her big win, regardless of it being preorchestrated, made her feverish to appraise every bit of her new territory. She looked over the railings at the half-beach, half-bay underneath. She patted masts as if she could gauge their sturdiness by doing so and hummed her approval.

When Madam Toy patted the topmast, Jack and Annie were jolted out of their destiny-sex spell and peeked through the slats of the crow's nest. Seeing Madam Toy again forced them to realize they'd really stepped in some shit. Jack struggled to wiggle his pants back up, thinking that if Madam Toy went back inside soon, they just might get away with it. But the bullet he'd pocketed earlier slipped out and dropped to the deck. It thudded and rolled around Madam Toy's feet. Jack and Annie shared a look that said they'd forgotten how hope could be broken. Madam Toy looked up, saw them in the crow's nest, and yowled, and the world skipped a beat.

The door of the main cabin swung open and slammed into the wall behind it, and Mei, Patrick, and Wayne came rushing out to the deck. Madam Toy's face turned pale and she looked right at Mei, eyes wide and fearful. They held each other's gaze, and what passed between them could only pass between allies. Wayne knew instantly that he'd been cheated; he knew they had to be working together. And when he finally looked up and saw Jack and Annie in the crow's nest, he knew this situation no longer involved him. He was insulted that he had been cheated, figured it out, and then felt too insignificant to bother doing anything about it. That was what happened when a victim's bully became a bigger victim. But Wayne silently promised himself he would get back at Madam Toy and Mei, and so began a suffocating obsession. He would find a way to get justice.

Jack did his best to hide his nerves from Annie as he

continued to struggle with his pants. He felt a boyish embarrassment for breaking the rules. He wasn't afraid of Madam Toy but was afraid for Annie. He had probably ruined her life; guilt flooded his mind. He'd been selfish, and now the thought of never having her again made him desperate for her. He hesitated to pull his socks back on, not ready to snuff out the fate that had found him. But eventually there was nothing left to do except climb down.

When they reached the deck, Madam Toy slapped Annie straight across the face, the kind of slap that only a woman who owned another woman could pull off. Sharp gasps came from Patrick and Wayne. Dolores crossed herself again. Madam Toy spat on the floor for good measure.

"What good are you now?" Madam Toy said. Her voice was thin and tired. "You are nothing."

The sense of exiting a dream came over everyone. Annie suffered the sting on her cheek without reacting and stared straight at Madam Toy. Madam Toy and Mei shared another look that seemed to pause time, and again Wayne saw it and knew that he had been cheated.

Jack and Annie left the ship without hesitating a moment longer. Patrick clapped his hand on Wayne's shoulder and guided him back to his fishing boat, because that felt like what should happen, and Dolores returned to the kitchen. Madam Toy and Mei stood on the deck a moment longer, then wordlessly parted—Madam Toy back into her new ship and Mei toward the lighthouse where, although the fire kept itself lit and did not need tending, she could be alone.

Mei walked up the lighthouse stairs, her legs heavy and weak. She opened the door to her living space, the room where the fire burned, and squinted in the sudden brilliance, a stark contrast to the deep night outside. The fire was burning high and orange, and the light of it was thrown against the angles of the room. All around there was gold—gold in blocks, nuggets, and dust, stacked, piled, and strewn; it was up the walls almost to the ceiling, dust floating and glimmering in the air and settling on the floor where inches of it already lay. The firelight made it shine and glitter, too bright, and it pulsed like a heartbeat.

In the beginning, Mei had admired the growing cache of gold in her lighthouse tower. She counted and weighed the gold she brought home, feeling with every addition that she must be getting close. Two thousand years spent in anticipation, waiting for something to happen, waiting to be whisked away to places unknown, had taken her from excitement to obsession, from a high to an illness.

She knew that whatever came next would be better than living here; she knew she was her own last hope. But knowing these things can only motivate a person for so long before it turns to madness. How quickly hope turns itself savage and starved.

None of this even mattered now; she had never come close to recollecting the debt that kept her here. Gold had appeared in the river at that sawmill, and as fast as a felled tree keels, the Gold Rush had begun. Suddenly there were people everywhere, standing knee-high in water day after day, swishing their pans around and around, the gentle scrape of silt on metal echoing and echoing, and the gold Mei had stolen so long ago, which she desperately needed to recollect, was getting dug up by the handful. It disappeared into the pockets of a population that swelled like an infection and was gone from her reach forever. She was trapped within her trap, hung on her own leash. Now, the gold gleaming all around her in the lighthouse mocked her. She was immensely wealthy, and she was immensely fucked.

Before, when playing mahjong in Chinatown, Mei had overheard two things, one right after the other, that created her plan. Which had unfolded tonight exactly as it should—until it didn't.

The first thing she overheard came from Mr. Zhou, who was known in Chinatown as the Gatekeeper since he was personally responsible for fixing the tickets of most of the Chinese here. Mr. Zhou was by nature an off-putting man. He was a salesman and a swindler, an obnoxious combination that made people pay higher prices just to make him go away. It was mysterious how someone so unlikable had gotten so much power, and Mr. Zhou knew every bit of what he had.

At the moment in question, Mr. Zhou was talking to a child, a boy of about five. He was telling the boy a story. Mei quickly recognized it as her own story—about how Gold Mountain only existed because she had put the gold there, and only now was it being discovered. She listened to him tell of her shame, of her journey across the Pacific Ocean to her lighthouse, and of the curse.

"So she can never leave?" the boy asked.

"Not until she gives back what she took," Mr. Zhou said.

"All the gold?"

"So the story goes," Mr. Zhou said, "depending on how you look at it. She took all that gold, but she also took a bride—herself—and wasn't that the whole point?"

Mei tensed at the question. She leaned closer to them. She felt as if Mr. Zhou must know she was here, listening, and that he spoke to her, not the boy. The boy looked confused.

"Is she in that lighthouse?" he said, pointing in the direction of the cliff.

"Some say she is," Mr. Zhou said. "There's no way of knowing."

"Can't they just go ask her?" the boy said.

"Would you admit to anyone that you were thousands of years old?" Mr. Zhou said. "That you were responsible for shaming an entire bloodline, for taking so much gold out of China and losing it?" He raised his eyebrows at the boy and smiled, then patted him on the bottom to run along.

Mr. Zhou, of course, would soon know who Mei was without knowing she was the lighthouse keeper. Mei would soon ask him to arrange for a girl—one from the same disgraced family he had just spoken of—to come here. He would find the request oddly specific, but Mei would offer enough money to make him keep his questions to himself. Mr. Zhou was not a man of many questions anyway.

Mei watched the boy scamper out of the room and into the sunlight. The mahjong tiles were mixed up, clicking against each other. She repeated in her mind what Mr. Zhou had said of her curse. *She also took a bride, and wasn't that the whole point?* She had never heard anyone say this before. *Depending on how you look at it* had never existed. She had never considered there being another way to look at it except that she had to find all the missing gold. And this made her feel stupid. The feeling of being exposed grew bigger inside her, and her breathing became shallow. She was used to hearing about herself, even took note of the ways her story shifted in its details over time, but she was not used to anyone understanding things better than she did. In storytelling, her curse was always just punctuation; for Mr. Zhou to ascribe logic to it made her feel brave and, soon, bold enough to come asking him for a favor. Perhaps Mr. Zhou was right. Perhaps there was another option. Perhaps it was the only option left because the Gold Rush, and all its people digging up her gold, had made it so.

The next thing Mei overheard came swiftly behind Mr. Zhou's story. At a different mahjong table, a woman told another woman that old Li Wei, who ran the butcher shop, had just had a girl show up on his doorstep—a girl from Guangzhou, of the Wong family—such a shame of a family—who had no money and no prospects and was a burden to old Li Wei and his business. Li Wei didn't know what to do with her; he did not want her or the scandal of the Wong family on his hands. He wanted someone to take her.

Mei bristled with uneasy excitement. She could take this girl and make her the bride to break the curse. This girl could be *the other way of looking at it*. The way the stories came like that, one right after the other, so easy, she feared that she had been found out and was quite possibly being duped. She looked around the mahjong hall. Mr. Zhou was turned back to the mahjong, a cigarette pinched between two fingers, studying the tiles in front of him. The two gossiping women paid no attention to anyone else and quickly moved on to a new topic, *tut-tut-ting* about a neighbor who sold second-rate ginger. No one noticed Mei, and, upon seeing the lack of threat in her surroundings, she let herself fully feel the hope of undoing her curse. She could leave her lighthouse for good and never have to look at another fleck of gold again.

Not an hour later, because all the best plans are made and executed without delay, she called on old Li Wei to find the Wong girl.

Wong Toy Lin was beautiful and young, and Mei felt a frenetic sense of relief when she saw her; when she offered to take her off Li Wei's hands, his relief was equally evident. Mei imagined the next steps would be easy, though she wasn't entirely sure what they were. She figured it all would sort itself out once she was able repay the debt. She assumed curses to be, in their own way, automated. She didn't need to know exactly how it worked; she would just know when it did. Wasn't that part of a curse? The not knowing, the powerlessness? If the curse could keep her here, it could surely let her know when it was time to leave.

When Mei asked Li Wei for Toy Lin, she imagined the girl would be grateful. But Toy Lin resented the idea of being taken off anyone's hands. She wasn't on anybody's hands but her own (and those of the white men who paid for the privilege). Toy Lin was no virgin and she was savvy about it. She'd made her own good money right underneath Li Wei's nose, and she did not need a strange woman to come rescue her.

Toy Lin made these things perfectly clear, but chancing upon the Wong bloodline felt significant and reassuring to Mei. Maybe Toy Lin couldn't break her curse, but she would make a good business partner. For the first time, Mei told someone who she really was. She couldn't explain why she trusted Toy Lin, but she did, and she felt like she was stepping up to the edge of a cliff by doing so, mesmerized by the view in front of her, terrified of the distance to the ground.

Then, when Jack's ship pulled into the harbor, Mei watched from the lighthouse as he built it into his public house. She watched him pour whiskey and shoot his gun and play poker all night long, and she knew it would have to be him, and it would have to be his ship and his table. Jack had the kind of listless sadness that kept him from noticing things, and his ship was positioned for surveillance. She went and made herself his dealer. She paid Mr. Zhou to bring her a girl. She gave Madam Toy the hand of cards that won. She had done everything right, but again she was back to nothing; another chance had been taken away. And here she was, alone in her gold-filled lighthouse.

Mei was calm in a way that even she herself found unnerving. She felt too tired to choose between rage and despair and so made herself hard like glass. She looked into the fire, the flames filling the lighthouse window, the glowing pile of embers beneath. The golden room flashed with a brilliant, mirrored flaring. The fire snapped and cracked. The heat swelled.

Mei closed her eyes and concentrated on the warmth against her skin. She breathed deep of the familiar smell of wood and char. She felt like she couldn't remember what had happened earlier, or maybe it was that she couldn't forget it, not for even a second of relief. She held an open palm over the fire and felt the heat between her fingers. She set her eyes on the patterns of fire eating around the logs and let her vision lose focus. She felt her mind clear. Then she pushed her hand down into the flames.

The heat sliced into her skin, but she forced herself to

keep her hand still. She cried out, knowing that the fire that roared and whipped like wind-filled sails smothered the sound. Her skin was rupturing. Her fingernails were tightening, then cracking apart. Her ears went cloudy and a low tone echoed through her head. A gust of cold, salty wind came through the window, and for a short second the flames receded, but they only surged back with greater life. Her knuckles blistered and splintered, bubbles of white skin rising, small wounds opening and chewing outward. The smell of burning skin, like meat on a spit, mingled with the smoke, and Mei's throat seized. Finally, she yanked her hand from the fire.

She inspected her burned hand—the deep ripples and blood and skin torn apart—and panted with the pain. The pain was the world. The burned skin looked like foothills from above, mounded and creased, like the ones she'd filled with stolen gold. She could see her flesh continue to cook. The smell was horrible and she struggled to choke back vomit. She went to the window, closed her eyes to the breaking dawn, and took deep, sucking gasps for air. When she steadied her breath moments later, there was no more pain. Her hand was unmarked, and the fire had put itself out for the night.

After Jack and Annie left the ship, they walked for miles

up the beach. They walked hesitantly, each waiting for the other to take the lead, though they never doubted that wherever they were going, they were going together. They walked side by side, his arm around her shoulders, and the shifting pressure of his limp against her kept time with her heartbeat. When they stopped, it was without knowing why, on top of a sand dune away from everything. They turned and looked back for the first time, and the Barbary Coast was nothing more than a glow smeared in the distance, the gas lamps converging with the lighthouse fire. They couldn't help feeling as if this new life had been awarded to them by mistake, that it was too easy; but they were happy, and happy was a better feeling to inhabit.

Jack spent the next few months building a little house for them. They learned that Annie had become pregnant that night in the crow's nest, and they were happier still, the kind of happy that never wonders why or how or when it will cease to be. They fell in love the way sand slips down a dune—delicately—because loving someone who is carrying a piece of you is the most uncomplicated kind of love.

Annie's body softened into curves, her face a bright, full moon. She rested her hand open-palmed over what she knew was a daughter. When the baby was born, she had a full head of dark hair and exactly ten unthinkably beautiful toes. She came out with her eyes closed and kept her eyes shut tight for weeks, as if she didn't want to belong to this world. When the baby did open her eyes, they were blue-black and bottomless as a starless sky. They named her Juniper.

They became a family and their hearts were full. They were complete. But they hadn't yet figured out that when they left Madam Toy's ship many months ago, they had left with a curse. Curses, like most things, beget more curses, and a cursed person will soon forget there is any other way. What is a curse but recognizing too much ease and edging some out? And so it had to be.

The Lighthouse Keeper gets up from her chair. You notice for the *first time that her feet are bare, and so caked in gold dust they look as though they're made of it. She has exactly ten toes. You check her hands—no scars or burn marks.*

She's back to moving around the room as if you're not there. You're not sure if she's taking a break or if she's finished. You feel a pang of worry and comb through what you've heard so far, fearing that if she is done, you've missed something.

Another curse? You came here to unravel one curse and now there is another, and you have no idea how the two are related. You replay the way she said it, try to measure her tone for a hint, but you can't discern any. There is too much there to sort out anything at all. She has kept herself on the periphery of her own story. You weren't prepared for her to tell you a story that isn't about her. It belongs to her, but it is not about her.

* * *

You read once that what you risk reveals what you value. If you value love, you risk heartbreak. If you value risk, you risk whatever you have of value. And if you value spite, you risk what others value. The words tangle in your mind. The disease of gambling has nuances you struggle to tease out. What is the difference between playing to win and playing for others to lose? The only one at that poker table who did not risk anything was Mei, but you know without knowing that that isn't true. You wonder what the risk is if you value a story.

She puts the kettle back on the grille. She uses an iron rod to reach into the fire and break the brittle logs into piles of ember. Then she puts three new logs on top. They snap and pop as they catch. The kettle whistles. You're beginning to calm down, reassured that the story isn't yet over. She brings the kettle to your seats and tops off both cups of tea. When she sits again, she does so with the kind of sigh that's full of time.

Fourteen Years Later

The moment Juniper was born was the moment Jack and Annie started to fade away. They were opposite ends of an hourglass. When she learned to walk, their legs became heavy. The longer her hair grew, the shorter theirs became. The first time she answered *I love you* was the last time she heard it. Every new thing that Juniper learned was erased from her parents' memories.

A thought for a thought. A word for a word. A grain of sand for a single moment.

Now, Juniper's hair was fourteen years long—long enough to weave a fishing net fit to catch a whale; so long that most of the length perpetually dragged on the floor behind her—and her parents were nearly bald. They hadn't moved or said a word in years. They deteriorated with each passing tide, their bodies thin and hollow, their skin like dust. Her mother was beautiful, once. Her father had a softly sad and handsome face. His hands were worn but soft and sometimes twitched while he lay there, like he was reaching for something.

For all fourteen years of Juniper's life, they had lived in the small house at the edge of the bay, with its one bedroom and an attic where she slept. The house was propped up on stilts on top of the sand dune, and it was slipping down, closer and closer toward the water's edge. The stilts reached fifty feet into the earth, sunk in holes that Jack had dug himself with only a trowel. But the sand wasn't going to let them stay.

Jack and Annie slept in a small bed perfectly in line with the front door. They lay on their backs, limbs tucked in tightly and bodies pressed gently together, their heads pointed to the shore. They were waiting for the house to slip all the way into the water so the tide would pull their bed out into the bay.

Their house was to the north of the Barbary Coast, where the dominant winds blew sharply past them. The Barbary Coast had grown threefold at least, and at night the gridlocked parade of ships glowed as if it were made of live coals spilled over from the lighthouse. Far from that mass of ships anchored in the shallows, Juniper had always been on the outside and learned about life through a spectator's eyes. She did very little. She spoke to very few. She imagined that the distant Barbary Coast was actually a hole in the earth where the world was swallowing itself, pulling ships from the wide sea into its open, ruby-lipped mouth. She admired it like one might admire such a thing. Which is to say, from far enough away, hell itself glitters like a goddamn showgirl.

In the autumn of her fourteenth year, Juniper awoke with her first period. Her underwear was wet with blood, and she felt sick and heavy and hot in a way she couldn't quite make sense of. She could smell herself, a new yet familiar scent, and it made her feel gross, like low tide. She was desperate to bathe. She slipped out of bed and down the attic ladder. In the living room her parents lay in their bed perfectly still, eyes closed. Juniper never knew anymore if they were asleep or awake. She hardly knew if they were alive unless she stopped and waited to hear them breathe, so moving around the house was now a series of pauses—step, pause, a rise and fall, continue. Their breathing was synchronized, and this morning it was heavier, harder to pull through the body. Juniper listened to three strained cycles of their breath, her heart pounding through the spaces between. She felt her own breath shorten, then quickly left for the beach.

Outside, the fog was densely poured into every crevice like it might caulk the ships in the harbor into place. The sun, low overhead, came through feeble and pale. The world felt impatient, the sun's thwarted efforts like restraint, and Juniper crossed the sand and waded into the water without undressing.

She floated on her back. The bay water made her feel better and seemed to help wash between her legs, a part of her she now thought of as a beached jellyfish you've just poked to find it is still alive. The water was metallic and everything above was heavy like buttermilk. A few gulls circled overhead like dribbled ink on a blank canvas. There was little wind. If Juniper remained perfectly still, she almost felt clean. She swam a little, putting her head under the water completely. She didn't see anyone approach, but when she came up, Mei was standing at the edge of the water.

Mei was the only person Juniper knew apart from her parents. She was the only person who knew Juniper existed at all, that her parents were slowly dying, that they would soon be underwater. Juniper knew her as protector, caretaker, and tender of the lighthouse. Mei was soft-spoken and smelled safe, like firewood. She brought food and things from the market in Chinatown; she cooked for Juniper, taught her, and loved her. She was as much a part of Juniper's life as the beach was its background. She always had been, and Juniper loved Mei like she wished she could love her mother.

Juniper waded back toward Mei at the water's edge. Her dress, heavy with water, stuck to her skin and made walking difficult. She was still feeling odd and weighed down. She squinted under the bright overcast sky. The chill of her wet clothes in the open air felt nice. She was grateful the sun was still hidden; there was only a small breeze to dry her. She told Mei about her period.

"That is wonderful news," Mei said. "You are a woman now."

Juniper flinched with embarrassment; it was an invasive thing to be told. Her heart dropped. She was a woman, and that came with a cost, but she had no idea what it might be. Her whole life, Juniper had carefully taken stock of what her actions cost her parents. But their hourglass was hard to predict and she could never find a pattern. The first time Juniper got a sunburn that made her skin dry like fallen leaves, Annie's skin became beautifully pale and bright. The first time Juniper read a love story, Jack's eyes leaked tears for days. Sometimes it seemed nothing had changed. Sometimes it seemed years passed in a moment. And now she asked herself: if she'd become a woman, how much time could possibly be left?

Though Juniper could barely remember anything else, things had not always been this way.

Once, Jack had carried her on his shoulders and waded into the bay. She held the sides of his head and laughed when the cold water covered her feet. Jack showed her how to reel in a crab basket, to peek inside and then pull it back to shore. He showed her how to look for scallops and mussels on wave-washed rocks, to dry seaweed, and to net small fish. Juniper took to the water and its life easily.

Once, Annie had taught her how to braid her hair. She showed Juniper how to section and weave, how to string shells or beads into the strands. The feeling of her mother's hands in her hair was the feeling of being both vulnerable and safe. The sound of the beads clicking together in her hair was the sound of magnets connecting.

Once, her childhood had seemed normal.

They were a family that was consumed with being a family. For many years Jack and Annie hardly put Juniper down, always keeping her in their arms, wanting almost to put her back inside them. They knew what was coming before she could even imagine it.

Juniper hadn't always slept in the attic. In the times before, each night Annie sat at Juniper's bedside in the room they all shared and told her stories of China. When she was done, Jack pulled the covers to Juniper's chin and kissed them both. As Juniper grew, Annie retold stories differently than she had before. A person's name was different, a happy ending turned sad, an enchantment turned into a curse. Juniper thought it was a private game between them, a test Annie was giving her to see if she could find the thing that had changed—as if, together, they were writing the truer version, the way things would really go. Juniper's world was as fluid as her mother's stories, the plot points slippery and easily reimagined, as they are in childhood. Her parents weren't losing their memory; they were free of margins. Until they weren't.

Juniper was four when she realized they were on opposite streams of time—that her parents were steadily disappearing as she grew. She tried to stop learning. To conserve time. She thought maybe they could go on existing in a kind of stasis, the hourglass knocked to its side to make two windless deserts, and live beside each other. But nothing stopped the steady leak.

Annie forgot her stories one by one. They flashed through and out of her memory with a final telling. When the last remaining one was forgotten, Annie came to Juniper's bedside and sat there vacant and confused.

Juniper held her hand—soft and spiritless as a sigh—and tried to prompt her into a familiar story. She said an opening line, hoping it would catch somewhere in Annie's mind. *Once upon a very long time ago, in a country where the river runs over a bed of pearls...* But the story was gone. Annie just sat and petted Juniper's hair for a little while, then left. Jack forgot to come to Juniper's bedside altogether.

Juniper moved into the attic. She couldn't bear to put herself to bed with their lost and devastated eyes watching her. It wasn't long before Jack and Annie stopped getting out of bed, and Juniper went to their bedside; she told them stories and kissed their foreheads. Sometimes their eyes stayed closed for days at a time. For that, Juniper felt relief. Their eyes were complicated. They held all the countless things they couldn't say. When their eyes closed for what she knew was the last time, she cried for days. She kept to the attic until she nearly starved, and then Mei came and saved her life.

Juniper's abdomen throbbed, and she stood before Mei with her arms around her stomach. She felt herself bleed, and it moved down her thigh underneath her dress. She stared down at the ground and strained to focus so she could see the distinct form of each grain of sand. She stared this way until the borders of her eyes hurt. She blinked, and the ground merged back into a uniform grey. If she never had to blink, she might be able to count them: pieces of a wide, uneven world where countless hourglasses were spilled. She looked down at the fractured shells in the sand and the chipped sand dollars with their narrow five-petal flowers like stars made of echoes. She kept her view of the world low, her feet and toes in the frame and her head bowed like a flower thirsty for rain.

"If I'm a woman, then it won't be long," Juniper said. "My parents will be gone soon. They are running out of time."

"Time only lasts until it doesn't," Mei said, which was what she always said. Maybe she thought it was a good thing to say. "Perhaps it's all spent," she added, though she'd never said that before.

"I stole it," Juniper said.

"Believe me," Mei said, "you are no thief."

Juniper looked back to the little house. She loved her home. Lonely children learn to feel the companionship that comes from the particular way the wind sings past a window or from the first sight of a colony of sea lions coming to grace the bayside each year. Her life at the beach had taught Juniper to see the nuances of change, the almost imperceptible things—a tree that's been pruned and now the view is wider; when young yellow flowers turn golden; age spots on the backs of her parents' hands, even when a drop of sunlight hadn't touched them. But the view from inside the hourglass was lifeless, its silence stifling, and there was no more nuance to the change approaching.

"Do you think they'll miss me?" Juniper said.

Mei's heart sank. She didn't know what the curse did to the mind, whether Jack and Annie could think or feel anything. Maybe they'd been missing their daughter all along. She didn't know which answer would protect Juniper more, and in this moment she wanted nothing more than to protect her.

"Of course they will," she said.

Juniper looked out over the water, feeling so full of thought that she was empty and so full of feeling that she was numb.

"Will you tell me a story?" Juniper said, wanting suddenly to imagine herself a part of another world. She was thinking about her mother and the lost stories, wondering if hearing one again might feel as sweet as it used to. She was thinking that *once upon a time* might finally be now, and finally something would begin instead of end.

The idea of telling Juniper a story felt dishonest. Mei did not tell stories. When one has been alive for millennia, there is no longer magic in the world. And what is a story without even a little magic? She'd heard the magic of her own story bloom and transform over time and found herself wishing for each new version she learned, only to be disappointed time after time. Eventually, she came to dislike stories altogether, even those that were not her own, seeing only the invention and none of the truth. Mei wanted to give Juniper the comfort she asked for but was frozen by the question. For the first time since telling it to Madam Toy, her own story was at the tip of her tongue. She could speak it: tell her story and tell that it was hers. But the words curdled in the hesitation.

"I am going to the market to get a few things," Mei said, ignoring Juniper's request. Her heart hurt. She would bring Juniper something for the pain and try to ignore her own, and she would do what needed to be done.

When the Lighthouse Keeper admits that her heart was hurt, you
feel closer to her, like she's confided in you. You want to recipro-
cate somehow; you want to make sure she keeps confiding, but
you sense that any outward gesture would spook this new amity
away. You decide the best thing to do is pretend you aren't there.
No eye contact, no words, no audible breathing. You can't help
but feel bruised thinking about Juniper—the burden of watching
a sad person be sad when they don't know or understand their
sadness is the most earnest kind of pity. You try to keep yourself
from imagining the person you love most fading away, then you're
struck by the fact that you are watching them fade away—as
they are you—because that is life. You hate it when that's life is
supposed to be an answer.

You break up your existential brooding and search the
Lighthouse Keeper's face. Her hair is pulled back into a large bun
the size of half a cantaloupe. It is very black with streaks of very
white. At times she looks aged; at others she looks as young and

beautiful as the girl she describes. Her skin is smooth but her eyes are weighted. Her lips suggest many lifetimes of being pursed, but they are relaxed now, slightly fallen, as if in disappointment. You want to know what she's feeling. You want to know if she knows you know she is Mei, and as you think it, you feel foolish for the comedic complexity of your curiosity. But you won't ask. You want her to keep going. You want to know what she did that needed to be done.

The walk from Juniper's little beach house to the Barbary Coast was one Mei took every day when she returned to her lighthouse. She would weave through Chinatown, then downtown, and then keep along the waterfront all the way to the red-light district, where Madam Toy's ship shone like a blood moon in a black sky even in the daytime, for it was always under the lighthouse's dick-shaped shadow.

As she approached Chinatown, the buildings became taller, houses stacked one on top of the other, teetering like spinning plates. Men smoked on the sidewalk; feathers of bluish smoke unwound from their buckled cigarettes, smelling like pencils and raw oats. Others sat on the steps in front of their houses, shelling seeds and nuts or peeling fruit with tiny pocketknives hidden in their palms and swishing fans made of wood and cloth at the flies. They held bags of vegetables high over their heads to show their neighbors and shouted to one another to trade.

Once Mei entered the marketplace, the air became warmer and thick with the smells of char and pepper and long-burning fires. There were people everywhere speaking in brusque Cantonese, crowded together but disconnected from one another, disregarding one another. They grabbed at merchants' produce and goods, held them to their noses, kneaded them with their fingers. They stood in the walkways and ate from bowls cupped underneath their chins. They chased and grappled for stray children, who shoved their hands between the bamboo ties of chicken cages. They stood among mounds of produce, barrels of beans and grains, browned birds hanging by their feet, stalls with fabric and clothes and fans or vases and teapots, shelves with jarred things, liquor, newspapers, flowers, and open barbecues. The clomping of horseshoes, the swish of fans, the pegging of walking sticks and canes, muffled clucks and shushing feathers, grunted haggling—it was everywhere all at once.

Mei moved through the marketplace in a practiced way. She moved quickly, ignoring everyone around her. She did not like the market and so avoided it as much as possible, but today she couldn't. She bought a bundle of kindling, a bag of long beans, and a pound of rice;

stopped to see the herbalist; and then went to find the fishmongers.

Wayne Jimbo and Patrick Christopher Michael O'Leary Laughlin sat on stools, surrounded by nets and bushels of shellfish and crates of iced fish, stacked and dripping. The smell of the ocean saturated the air around them. Wayne's face was wind-chapped and stiff, his narrow eyes unfocused. He looked old: the fifteen years since Mei had seen him up close were worn into the slope of his shoulders. Patrick, who wore a wool cap that didn't contain his twine-like hair, looked old, too, sitting there without a drop of light in his face.

Mei had seen them at the market before, many times, but had kept a great distance until now. She hesitated behind the guilt that came when she saw just how much they'd aged; she'd never before recognized her own responsibility in the matter. But she was standing in front of them, staring, and they were staring back; it was too late to change her mind.

"What'll it be this morning?" Patrick said, because he didn't know what else to say and he didn't want to sit there stuck in her gaze forever. His voice was scratchy, lilting and askew in the way he said *morning*.

"I am here for Madam Toy," Mei said, breaking her stare and looking into her hands. "I will take her usual order and deliver it myself."

Patrick pulled a crate closer and shoveled two handfuls of oysters into a sheet of paper that he then wrapped up like an envelope and tied with string. The mere mention of Madam Toy made him feel tense and exposed; he would much rather hand the oysters over now than deliver them. He moved quickly and methodically but stole glances at Mei, trying to place the familiarity of her face. Her hands.

Wayne felt his neck go hot and his ears fuzzy. He knew her immediately. He felt many things and showed none, as one does when they've seen a ghost. He was moving back in time. He knew Madam Toy and Mei were working together. He'd known it all along. They had cheated him, ruined him, and all his indignation came hurtling out of its long dormancy.

For the first few years after that fateful night of poker, Wayne's resentment had nagged at him. From the fishing boat, he studied the ship and its steady transformation in Madam Toy's hands. He refused to go with Patrick to deliver her oysters but speculated and observed from afar. He'd searched for Mei's face in crowds. He'd scanned the northern beach with a spyglass and seen the faraway silhouettes of Jack and Annie at their little house. They had a baby. They were happy. Just as he thought: He'd done Annie a favor. He was the one who'd made her happy. Wasn't that good enough?

Wayne tried to give up his obsession with being cheated and move forward with the monotony of a fishing boat on still water. He kept himself from spying as best as he could and attempted to persuade himself to forget, which he had kind of done, almost, until now. Now his mind raced, reaching for the imaginary revenge schemes he'd spun long ago.

"Free of charge, of course," Patrick said as he held the package out to Mei, then immediately turned his attention to another customer.

With the oysters in hand, Mei met Wayne's stare for just a second, and they both knew what they both knew.

Mei hurried away. She felt flustered and regretted going to the fishmongers at all. She'd wanted to bring the oysters to remind Madam Toy that they were still bound by an unfulfilled promise. Fifteen years had passed without a word between them, though Mei was still owed Madam Toy's help. She still thought Madam Toy's was the safest place to keep Juniper. She walked faster, wanting to forget the look on Wayne's face and the sinking feeling that she'd just messed everything up.

Layers of the market peeled from Mei as she walked along the waterfront. The strong, sticky smells, the chaos of noise and language, the hasty rhythm and its temper: one by one these things were pared from her senses, and the *pat-pat* of her feet was all she listened to until she reached Madam Toy's ship.

Madam Toy's ship was known as the *Fortune Lookie*, and Madam Toy was known as the matron of its china dolls and their bite-size sex appeal. There was not one red light but many paper lanterns, lit even in the daytime, strung all the way around the railing of the main deck. There was a quiet and empty feeling while the girls who lived there slept until the moon rose.

Mei walked right into the kitchen, where Dolores held a large bowl pinned against her hip and stirred its contents with a wooden spoon. Mei set the bundle of oysters down and waited for Dolores to recognize her, but whether she did or not was unclear. Dolores either did and didn't care or didn't and didn't care, and before there was any more to say about the reunion, Madam Toy's voice broke the silence.

"I wasn't sure I would see you again." Madam Toy looked Mei over the way one might regard a line of ants at the cupboard—somewhere between distressed and inconvenienced.

Mei wasn't sure what to say. Before, when Mei found Madam Toy at old Li Wei's butcher shop, they had been friendly with one another. They were relatives by long past ancestry and by the village, so they were each other's only family. They understood their friendship as the result of Mei's rescuing. Madam Toy had been poor and without potential; Mei had a plan to change that, and that made her the proprietor of Madam Toy's future.

When Jack and Annie came down from the crow's nest, there was a shift in the relationship. It was Madam Toy's fault that this had happened, and an intense guilt came over her. She had squandered the best chance Mei had had in her many lifetimes, and she knew it. She felt light-headed as she struggled to understand and pan-icked that she would lose everything else too. She didn't really care about Annie or her ruined virginity; that had all been for Mei. The entire thing was for Mei. Really, she had been doing Mei a favor. Mei was the one who needed her. In a single moment, Madam Toy's guilt morphed into denial and then resentment, and Mei went from savior to parasite.

"Why don't we sit," Madam Toy said, still unreadable. She went into the main cabin and took a seat at the poker table, which was no longer a poker table but the sort of cash register of the place. They sat across from one another and they were strangers. Madam Toy knew noth-ing of Juniper or what had become of Jack and Annie; she hadn't given Wayne another thought and only spot-ted Patrick occasionally when he brought the oysters to

Dolores. She had not expected to see Mei suddenly back on her ship.

"I take it you need my help again?" Madam Toy said.

"I'm owed your help," Mei said. "I have a girl, and I need you to keep her safe for a while."

"She is not safe with you?"

"She has no home. If I take her to the lighthouse, she will find out. You only need to care for her for a few days. Until Mr. Zhou comes and I can send her off."

"You're sending the girl back to China?" Madam Toy said.

"I've asked him to take her there," Mei said. She paused. "I'm not sure."

And she wasn't sure, not about what to do, nor about whether or not to do it. Her mind was stuck between unknowns. It made sense to her—she'd left China, so Mr. Zhou, who'd brought the Wong bloodline here, should take Juniper back to China in her place—but Mei could not make sense of how her body was suddenly feeling so hollow, carved out with guilt. She felt tricked—like she'd been given the wrong answers to questions she didn't ask but should have. Madam Toy interrupted her thoughts.

"You say care for her, but we are not here to care about this girl," Madam Toy said. "You need to keep this girl a virgin and you want to bring her *here*? Why?"

Mei had forgotten why, or perhaps there never really was a why. Madam Toy was woven into her story now, and she had never unwoven her. But what Madam Toy said—*We are not here to care about this girl*—plagued Mei with the heavy threat of something that had too easily slipped her notice. She was not supposed to love Juniper. But she'd never known to know better.

When Jack and Annie lost the ability to walk and talk, Mei finally went to their little house on the beach. When Juniper came down from the attic where she hid, Mei felt like she was the one who'd been chosen. Juniper was a sweet child. She was very intelligent—privately—and very shy. There weren't any people to be shy around, so she was shy within her own mind. She was only bold in how much she needed Mei. Mei didn't know how much she needed to be needed, and so she'd fallen in love with Juniper from that first starved look. Mei loved Juniper so simply that it was impossible to know it as a choice, and they belonged to the love between them.

She had refused the thought of using Juniper for her freedom until she didn't think it anymore at all. But now it was here: Juniper was a woman and it was time. Time was something Mei had been fighting for two thousand years, and it was going to be unfrozen now, just when she'd started to like the cold. She could change her mind, but she could change nothing else if she did. She was afraid, and she needed someone like Madam Toy to help her move forward.

The fog was spilling into the bay and hung over the open water. The tide was high and licking at the stilts of the little house on the beach. The sand between the door and the water's edge was damp, the threshold waterlogged. Juniper's clothes were soaked and coated in wet sand. Her hands were blistered from furiously digging out another trench.

Every day for the last few months, Juniper had spent the afternoon digging a trench around her house, hoping that when the tide finally did come up, it would be diverted. The trench was two feet deep, but every time the tide receded, it was left collapsed and muddy. And every time, Juniper dug it again. She had only an old trowel to use and so remained always on her knees as if in unfinished prayer.

Water spilled into the trench. Juniper tossed the trowel away and used her hands to scoop out the water and loose silt. Her weight on her knees pushed more sand in. She couldn't clear much out before the next wave slipped over the beach and into the trench. The tide was coming earlier today and it was rising fast. There was nothing more to do.

Juniper got to her feet, light-headed after kneeling for so long. The pain in her stomach came again as she stretched upward. She felt hot, though she had goose bumps up and down her arms from the wet and wind. From behind the house she saw Mei approaching.

"Juniper, you should be inside," Mei said.

Mei was carrying a bag that Juniper recognized as coming from the market. Juniper was relieved to see her and suddenly felt like crying. She hurried over to Mei, threw her arms around her waist in a desperate hug, and held on. Mei dropped her bag and embraced Juniper, and they stood that way for a long moment. When they let go, Juniper crossed her arms over the pain in her belly.

"I brought you something to eat," Mei said. "And I brought you some tea from the herbalist. It will stop the pain."

Mei handed the bag to Juniper, who held it with a heavy arm, straight down her side.

"Are you leaving?" Juniper asked. Some nights, Mei stayed. They'd build a fire on the beach and cook together and eat outside. They'd feel like they were doing things right for life to be so good. It wasn't often and was always a surprise, but today, Juniper couldn't help feeling rejected.

"I'm sorry, Juniper, I can't stay," Mei said, and she really felt sorry. And then she felt the sobering foolishness of feeling sorry. "Make some tea and go to bed. You'll feel better." Then she walked quickly away.

The front door to the little beach house, swollen from the water, stuck when Juniper tried to open it. She threw her shoulder against it and it popped open with a splintering sound. The floor inside was damp. She forced the door closed behind her, then stood in the entryway, her hair and clothes dripping. Her stomach wrenched with pain. She went to Jack and Annie's bed, gave each of them a kiss on the forehead, and then sat down where Annie's legs were tucked underneath the blankets. She listened to them breathe. The sound, thin and stretched, made Juniper feel as though she were out of breath too. She no longer felt like crying. She felt tired, tired of their complicated game, tired of time funneling out of her parents. She'd always been afraid of them dying, but now she was calm.

Juniper left a big wet spot when she got up from the bed. She didn't feel like eating. Her stomach hurt, and the ache overtook any suggestion of hunger, though she was feeling faint. She changed her clothes and put rags in her panties for the blood. She made a cup of the tea Mei had brought for her and took it up to her bedroom. She drank it looking out her window at the budding city on the other side of the bay, where faraway oil lamps shone orange against the deep green hills. Her body relaxed. Her mind slowed into deep sleep. Then the high tide came flooding into the little beach house and carried them all away.

You look down at your teacup and seriously question whether or not it's poison. You take a moment to assess if you're feeling funny. You aren't. In fact, you're feeling the kind of comfort that only a good story can give. The Lighthouse Keeper's words are sliding through the air and taking form to reveal another world that belongs only to this moment. You realize how wrapped up you are. You want to tell her that it's a good story, that you like it, but you also don't want to say anything at all, because you haven't yet said anything and the silence feels like an agreement now. That, and you see dimness and shame on her face that wasn't there before. She shifts in her chair. She adjusts the blanket in her lap. She takes a sip of tea. You realize how empty the room is without her voice, and the story's moment begins to dissolve. Again, you worry that this is the end. You know it's not, but you can't help feeling threatened.

You take another big gulp from your teacup—to prove your trust—and sit as still as possible. You pretend to find the teacup *fascinating so as not to pressure her with too much attention. There are little green granules of tea leaves collected at the bottom of the cup, and perhaps little bits of gold dust too. The ceramic is still warm, even though the tea is half gone. You sneak a glance at the Lighthouse Keeper; her eyes are closed. She has the expression of one thinking about feelings. You consider making a noise to rouse her, but you're too fearful of distracting her. So you wait, anxiously, feeling like you're digging a flooded hole, until she opens her eyes with a deep inhale and continues.*

Juniper woke up with a start—the way your entire body says *what the goddamn fuck* when it's been roused too suddenly—to a creaking whine coming from pulley spools above her head. She saw the ropes moving, one up, one down. She sat up gasping, afraid, then had the distinct sensation of falling. She saw nothing but the morning's dense white fog above, around, and below her. She was completely alone, suspended. She'd woken up in the crow's nest of the old wooden ship, Madam Toy's *Fortune Lookie*, though she did not know that this was that ship, or that this was the ship her own father had called home, the very one where her life became collateral. She couldn't see anything but fog and the wooden railings around the tightly confined crow's nest, but knew in her body that she was high up in the air.

The creak of the pulley came in staccato shifts of switching hands. Juniper moved as far away from it as she could, which was not far at all, and tried to hide behind the topmast. She felt dizzy and weightless crouching on top of the infinite twists of her long, long hair, which formed a pile beneath her like an unbound hay bale. She searched the fog, waiting for something to come into focus. A tray appeared from below her, rising on the pulley, and stopped right beside the railings of the crow's nest. There was a bamboo steam basket of food on it; the heat cleared a pocket of air around it where the fog faded. Juniper left the basket on its tray and stayed as far as possible to the other side of the topmast, watching like one might watch a coiled snake, keeping the basket in her peripheral vision while never looking directly at it.

The crow's nest was its own world. Juniper remained as still as she could. Around her on the floor, buried underneath her sprawling hair, was a pile of heavy woolen blankets and a small pillow; there was a pail filled with fresh water, a lidded chamber pot, and clean rags for her period—too intimate of a detail to ignore. The only thing Juniper did know about the crow's nest was that she was intended to stay for a while.

When the fog did clear, it was almost afternoon, and Juniper got her first real look at San Francisco from above.

From the crow's nest she could see in every direction for miles. The rounded hills, green and stippled with yellow flowers; the severe drop of cliff and crag on the northern coastline; the bay, rolled out wide like a spread fan—it was all beautiful, so much so that Juniper thought maybe she was a guest, not a prisoner. This idea passed quickly when she looked below to the Barbary Coast.

Some of the ships huddled so close together that boards had been laid between them as untidy walkways, and a few dusty-looking people were roaming the nearby decks and piers. The ship beneath the crow's nest looked brittle and trodden, the decks empty. It was set in front of all the other ships in the harbor, closest to the cliffside, a victor or a leper—it was hard to tell. Juniper had seen these ships her whole life from her little house on the beach, but she'd never thought about being aboard one. Though she knew they must belong to somebody, she had never thought of anyone at all being aboard them except for the sailors who'd brought them here. To Juniper, the ships always seemed to be forgotten, the way a shell is abandoned when its snail moves on. She thought of them as fossils.

The lighthouse was fully in view when the fog pulled away. It was quite close to the ship. Juniper was surprised by its massiveness and by how gloomy it looked in the daylight. Its distinct phallic shadow lay over the ship, but Juniper was above it. She was close to the height of its open, encircling window, grey and dark. By now, Mei might know she was missing. Mei would come for her. She just had to wait.

Juniper didn't see anyone on the ship all day long. She was very bored. She tugged on the pulley rope, but it was tied at the bottom of the mast and didn't budge. She opened the basket Madam Toy had given her to find a pile of rice, dried strips of seaweed, and boiled eggs. She didn't feel hungry at all, so she closed it again. She thought about shouting for help but decided she'd rather reserve the possibility of being forgotten up there. She thought about how she could get down, then uneasily about what might be waiting for her on the ground.

She stood and circled the edge of the crow's nest, first in a determined way, then idly, looking down from every possible angle. She tugged at the pulley ropes again, but they were securely tied. The step rungs had been removed from the topmast altogether. There was no way down, and now her hair had wrapped around and around the topmast from the circles she'd paced, so she was completely tethered in place with only enough slack to sit and try to untangle it. However, getting her hair sorted was impossible without a comb, and the wind kept it flapping about, so at last Juniper just sat and stared at the lighthouse, keeping her eyes fixed on the wraparound window. Every once in a while, a bird's shadow passed over it and hope prickled inside Juniper's skin, but it was always nothing. Nothing moved inside the lighthouse.

Mei watched Juniper sitting in the crow's nest from her lighthouse. She stayed far back enough from the window to keep her shape and shadow from sight. The fact that Juniper never yelled or waved her hands made her heart hurt; Juniper was going to just take it without question. The way Juniper just stared and stared into the lighthouse made it even worse.

Mei felt the need to explain herself. She wanted to provide good answers to all of the questions Juniper must have. She still wanted to protect her, and most of all she wanted to forget why she was protecting her in the first place. She hoped she could forget when it was all done.

When the sun began to drop, the sky faded to its palest silvery blue. The bay was almost the same tone, the land around was dark, and the streetlamps glowed deep yellow. The fog was coming in—fast—the way the high tide finds and floods the gullies between sand dunes. It swallowed the crow's nest altogether, and Paloma, the ship's caretaker, felt a little bad for the girl who was trapped up there. She unwrapped the pulley rope from its tie-down and hoisted a new basket of food up to Juniper. When it reached the top, Juniper made no move to take it; this annoyed Paloma. Paloma was often annoyed, and even more so since this girl had appeared and made her list of chores longer. Paloma had yellow hair and a body quite like a cauliflower; she looked odd among the other girls on the ship, like a duckling that had mistaken the cats for its family.

It was getting chilly on deck; the wind had picked up. 87 "You have to take it!" Paloma shouted blindly straight upward into the fog, even though she'd been told not to talk to Juniper. She figured it was okay if they couldn't even see each other, and she wasn't about to just stand around and wait. She shook the ropes a little; they slapped against the mast and jiggled the tray.

The motion startled Juniper and she took the basket, her resolve folding quickly.

"You have to put the other one back, too!" Paloma shouted.

Juniper had waited all day for a sign of human presence, but now she felt too rushed. She couldn't bring herself to say anything to the disembodied voice, so she just followed directions. She put the other basket, still full, onto the pulley tray. Down it went, the spool creaking as it turned, and at the bottom, the rope was tied in place.

The crow's nest was uncomfortably small. The only way for Juniper to lie flat on her back would have been with the topmast between her legs, which she found a bit crude. Instead she had to lie on her side and bend to the curve of the nest, forced into a fetal position. She dragged the pillow underneath her head, still held close to the mast by her hair. She missed her parents and felt ashamed that this was the first time she'd thought about them all day. Perhaps her parents were dead, their hourglass empty once and for all.

She pulled the blankets over her. The unfavorable reality of sleeping outdoors at the top of a tall pole in the wind and the blindness sank in. The only thing she could see through the dense fog was the faintest glow of the lighthouse fire. She didn't see the men that came onto the ship, but she sensed them. She sensed them like one senses being snuck up on—a stray, misjudged footstep cutting through the silence, a door swinging closed and shaking in its frame, a fuzziness around the ears to portend a crowd.

Paloma took the first basket from the pulley and retied the rope. The basket was untouched—the boiled eggs stiff and cold, the dried seaweed dampened, the rice dry. The day before, when Madam Toy had informed Paloma of the mysterious girl in the crow's nest and told her not to talk to her, she had also warned Paloma not to eat any of the food in those baskets. But Madam Toy often told Paloma not to eat; this was no different. Her entire life on the Madam's ship was lived on table scraps. And it seemed to Paloma like such a warning about the food applied specifically to the food going *up* to the crow's nest, not to the cold, wasted leftovers. So she ate the eggs and rice.

Then she brought the empty basket to the kitchen where Dolores, the kitchen hand, was stirring something in a bowl pressed to her hipbone. The room was dense with smoke and the smell of pork fat on hot cast iron. Paloma put the basket near the wash pit and slipped through the swinging doors to the main cabin.

From outside, Madam Toy's *Fortune Lookie* drew hardly any notice. Despite the red lanterns, eyes had a tendency to skim over its shadows. It had never fully shed its air of abandonment, but this was purposeful, so as to attract only those who could see in the dark. Inside, it was an entirely different place. The bar in the main cabin was crowded, sticky, and covered in glasses both empty and full, cigarette butts, and candle stubs. Underneath a brass chandelier, too many small circular tables were jammed together too closely, so that everyone who sat knocked knees. The room was lit with heavy, dim red light; the air was opaque with tobacco smoke, sweetly perfumed, and offensively warm. Red scarves were tacked over the portholes and draped over the lamps, and fans and scrolls hung on the walls. It had an Oriental look, though with a slight nautical theme, given all of the repurposed props—an anchor against a wall, barrels pushed into corners, piles of rope and netting.

The only clearing in the room was against the back wall, where there was a fireplace and a mantel decorated with ragged playing cards, hand fans, and more candle stubs. This clearing, marked off by a border of rowboat oars, served as a stage, and beside the stage was Madam Toy's table, the old poker table she'd taken right from under Jack fifteen years before. She sat all night long at her table, leaning back, relaxed, in a large and cushioned chintz armchair.

Paloma tiptoed around, picking up empty glasses to be washed. Though it was pretty early in the night, the ship was crowded with men. They sat at the small tables holding glasses of whiskey in one hand and tugging at their crotches with the other; they watched Madam Toy's Oriental girls parade across the stage in stockings and corsets like little dolls sewn from the same pattern. When a girl struck a man's fancy, he went to Madam Toy's table and dropped coins or bits of gold in her hand, which she shoved down into her bosom. Then he followed the girl down into the belly of the ship where she might sit in his lap, nuzzle his neck, wiggle her tits on his face, maybe even give his willy a squeeze. He could pay more to touch her back. He could pay even more than that to put her on her back.

Paloma moved through the room as invisibly as she could. She didn't want to be grabbed by any of the men, which generally happened when the thing they wanted to grab was just out of reach. She'd been on Madam Toy's ship for a few years now. She knew that her place as the ship's caretaker was earned by her lack of appeal, and that invisibility was best.

Paloma's mother was dead, her life traded for that of her fifth child. It was Paloma's father who'd brought her to the Barbary Coast when she turned fourteen. He was poor; that was all Paloma really knew about the man. He'd been gone all day, drunk at night, and poor. And he'd never wanted her. They had lived in the valley's farmland, in the orange groves, at least a full day's journey from the bay.

Her parents had been expecting a boy. When Paloma came out of the womb, they both lamented the surprise, and she slipped through her father's hands and hit her head on the floor. She still had a rosy blotch on her forehead, flat like a skipping stone. She found this story symbolic in a precedent-setting way.

When she reached marrying age, her father tried bribing all the men he knew to take her, but he had little for a dowry. And Paloma talked too much. She told stories—funny stories—and gossiped more than a lady should, and she was not at all pretty. After that, her father spent a brief time trying to push her into the nunnery, but the Church was not a place for funny girls either. She might have the looks of someone whose best shot was to marry the Lord, but not the mouth.

Eventually, Paloma's father brought her to the Barbary Coast in a carriage full of oranges and left her there standing in the street as he rode back to the valley. She knew she would never see him again, which was fine, but she would also never see her sisters again. She wished she'd brought them with her; they would be better off with her. The guilt of leaving them behind, as much as it wasn't her fault, would never leave her. But she was here now, and there was nothing else to do but start talking herself into a better situation, which she did when she came to Madam Toy's ship.

Madam Toy's was not the first door Paloma had knocked on hoping to make a deal to work for a bed, but it was the first one that let her in. It was also the first door belonging to a Chinese person and the first Chinese person Paloma had ever seen. She had thought that perhaps she might have some power around the Chinese, being white and all, but Madam Toy immediately made clear that this was her ship, and she was its goddamn queen.

There was a short while that Madam Toy had Paloma strip for the men just like her Chinese girls, but it didn't last long. Her small nose, angled like a diamond, her chin, square and forward, eyes too far apart, and blonde eyebrows lost on a constantly flushed face just didn't do it for the men. Madam Toy didn't make any money off of Paloma, and she took the heckling more personally than Paloma did. Besides, Paloma's whiteness really hurt the whole Oriental feel. So Madam Toy somewhat begrudgingly let Paloma stay on as the ship's caretaker, working beside Dolores to make the business run. Again, Paloma was a burden, although she had that in common with Madam Toy's past life, and the truth was that Madam Toy needed Paloma just as much as Paloma needed her. Somebody had to do all the work around there.

Paloma went back to the kitchen to wash the glassware. Dolores, who was still stirring something in that big bowl with her knotted hands, gave a small nod to Paloma while continuing her fluid rosary whispers—grace, fruit, mother, sinner—which she prayed every night before she retired for bed. Paloma was hungry. She would have to eat whatever Dolores could find that she could throw in a pot and call food, most commonly a sort of stew made of rice bloated like cotton, boiled oatmeal, potato skins, and mysterious scraps of gristle. Tonight, perhaps fueled by the remnant taste of the eggs she'd stolen earlier, the sight of that stew really pissed her off. Of course, she ate it anyway and went to bed angry.

You see a shadow of confrontation on the Lighthouse Keeper's
face, a pleading crease between the eyebrows. Her voice comes
from a different stance now, like she's come out from behind the
camera to rearrange the shot. It's a need to explain herself, you
think, and you wonder if the version she's telling is one that's been
altered to justify her own role in it. Or perhaps you're hearing the
stale desperation of being unable to alter or justify. Or perhaps
justify isn't the right word at all and it's really more about feeling
Paloma's feelings, as any good storyteller would. You decide you
like Paloma. You've been craving her—the way she makes light of
dark, noise of obedience. You didn't realize you were getting tired
of helplessness until she came into the story.

You imagine what being in a crow's nest might feel like, and
when you look out the window your body has that swooping
reminder of being high off the ground. You think about stories
of towers and the girls they hide from the world. And of towers
where girls are not hidden but lay bare. For the second time, the

Lighthouse Keeper rises and stokes the fire. This time she only puts one new log on, and you feel a stab of something like loss; can the story really be winding down?

The log catches with little snaps and a fuzzy, steamy sound. The flames recede while they work on the fresh wood and all the light in the room is reduced to what's thrown by the embers. You let your eyes blur the orange glow and imagine it is all the light in the world. It's an odd feeling, being in a place with only a fire for light and knowing that there'd be nothing but blackness without it. You've never realized how abstract darkness has become. You conjure the fear you would feel if you were Juniper. How strange and humiliating to be kidnapped into silent dependency—though if you'd lived your entire life that way, what was a crow's nest? What was yet another person who couldn't talk to you, or being bound to the unyielding by your hair?

The Lighthouse Keeper retakes her seat. You have spun yourself into an attitude of confrontation like hers, but now she appears calm. The look of pleading has given way to gravity. She's changed her stance again and stepped back behind the camera.

⚓

The sound of the creaking pulley spool woke Juniper up with a charge that vibrated like a tuning fork. It was too foggy to see the deck below, but soon the next basket of food peeked through as it came up. Wanting to make the situation go away as quickly as possible, Juniper exchanged it for the last untouched basket of scallops and long beans. She saw, fastened to the lid of the basket, a comb, which made her feel both relieved and uneasy. When she heard the tray reach the bottom, followed by Paloma's footsteps across the deck, she checked the rope. It was tied again.

Paloma's annoyance at finding another uneaten basket was curbed by a powerful hunger, and any hesitation over Madam Toy's instruction not to eat Juniper's food had departed. Everything was cold and had lost its original texture, but it was better food than she ever got. Paloma ate in big bites as she walked back to the kitchen but didn't make it inside before Madam Toy came out onto the deck. Paloma shoved what was left in her hand into her mouth, put the lid back on the basket, wiped her hand on her hip, and tried to hurry past with her head down.

"Paloma," Madam Toy said.

Paloma chewed as fast as she could. When she finally turned to answer, the Madam grabbed her chin and pinched her cheeks together. She squeezed until Paloma's lips parted. Half-chewed scallops and long beans floated over her tongue. Madam Toy's grip made it so she couldn't chew or swallow; she yanked Paloma forward by the chin and said, "Spit it out."

Paloma let the glob of wet, mashed food fall from her

mouth onto the deck. Madam yanked her chin again. She held Paloma's face close to hers, beneath hers. Paloma could smell the tea on her breath, the salt water on her hands.

"I told you not to talk to her," Madam Toy said. She did not gesture nor look to the crow's nest, but Paloma knew what she meant. "Stupid, ugly girl," Madam Toy said, and let go. Before Paloma could get away Madam Toy added, "Clean this up," and pointed at the spit-soggy food.

Paloma hurried inside to start her chores. She would clean up her mess, but she would let it sit there awhile first. Downstairs, she stripped the beds and gathered stockings and panties and nighties from the bedroom floors. She hated doing the laundry. She hated the scent of a girl covered with sweet and flowery perfume, and she hated the way the smell of a man mingled with it.

But Paloma did like knowing that she could wash it all away, erase the last guest from the sheets. These sheets would soon be occupied with another man's greed. They would accept another life, another smell, another kind of sweaty warmth, at least for a while. And for Paloma, the fact that she could wad up all that symbolism in her arms made her feel pretty good. It made her feel like one day she could just leave, and this life of hers would be erased in the laundry. She would leave as soon as she could steal enough money, which she hadn't come close to doing yet, for when there is sex to be bought, men keep close track of their cash. That, and Madam Toy kept all her money in her bra.

The laundry was done on the main deck, where a barrel of warm, soapy water that Dolores prepared sat waiting. Paloma shoved all of the laundry into the barrel, pushing it down until it sank in the water. Then she went about setting up the laundry lines—the ship's riggings that she crossed and refastened into a web. She'd long ago figured out a pattern that worked, though the first time she'd tried it, she made a real mess out of the rigging. Madam Toy had to call in a sailor to fix the ropes and punished Paloma with no food for five full days. Paloma considered that to be the start of the war between her and Madam Toy. Since then, Paloma had often been punished with missed meals, but she hadn't starved yet; Dolores, being the Samaritan she was, always gave Paloma a spoonful of rice for every prayer she agreed to recite.

When the lines were set up, Paloma climbed over the rim of the soap-water barrel and plunged all the way inside. It was an awkward task, and she had no other way to do it if she wanted to avoid a spill and a scolding. It was also a good opportunity to take a little bath, which she did not often get.

Paloma bobbed up and down, trampling the laundry in the barrel. Her feet made wet slurping sounds that echoed. She liked to imagine Madam Toy's face beneath her feet, but really, it was home that came to mind. It was the farmland on the verge of flood. It was her father, too drunk to stand, and she and her sisters dragging sandbags from the barn to catch topsoil runoff. It was wet ankles, the feeling of loss, and the persistence of heavy rain. This was what she hated most about the laundry.

When everything was washed, Paloma put it inside a basket that she dragged alongside the laundry lines as she hung it all to dry. She forced herself not to even look toward the crow's nest. The loose clothespins in her apron pocket rattled every time she reached for a new one, and as she stretched up to pin them, rills of water ran the length of her arm underneath her sleeve—an unpleasant feeling. But she was grateful there was no wind. It was early afternoon when she finished, and the sun was finally out in the clear sky and at its highest point. The hanging bedsheets created a maze of walls. The clothes made the ship resemble a sort of ghostly gallows—small, girlish garments floating like headless paper dolls—the scattered remnants of a purgatory sentence served.

Since the moment Juniper had seen the comb early that morning, she'd been working on untangling her hair from the topmast. When her arms became too tired to continue, she took a break and watched Paloma in the riggings, with her yellow hair and wide shoulders, tying all of the laundry in place and getting lost in the maze of hanging bedsheets. Juniper decided against shouting; she felt so defenseless and trapped by her hair. It took hours to unwrap herself enough to even stand. Her hair had twisted around the mast in both directions and tangled around the entire perimeter. As she worked, she got stuck in odd postures trying to reach the ends. She brushed with short strokes until her arms were too tired again. She paused to pull hair out of the comb and drop it off the side of the crow's nest. She looked over at the lighthouse, then kept combing, moving up the length of her hair, which was dozens of arms' lengths long, but the wind put it back in disarray before she could make much progress.

Meanwhile, Wayne and Patrick sat in their rowboat in the bay, a few ships away from Madam Toy's. The sun was going down, and the air had dramatically cooled since the afternoon. Patrick threw a net into the water, let it sink, then slowly reeled it in; a few fish flopped, caught in its weave. Wayne had not touched any fishing gear all day but had perched at the edge of the boat, sweeping his spyglass across the *Fortune Lookie*. He caught sight of

Madam Toy once, and a squat girl who was outside doing the laundry. There was nothing else.

He was ready to give up but then not ready at all and continued his inspection of the ship as night fell. The lighthouse fire caught and broke into bright flames, and this pulse of light illuminated something he'd failed to see before: a figure standing in the crow's nest. Wayne felt like he was not entirely in his body. He felt like a wisp of the fog that was beginning to drift in—ghostly fog, like the girl in the crow's nest (though Juniper was a ghost who didn't know she was a ghost, which made her more of a shadow).

Wayne shoved his spyglass into Patrick's hands, causing him to drop the net and its few fish back into the water, and pointed to the crow's nest. He did not know how to say what he saw. It was Annie. She was on the ship. He swore it; but no, it couldn't be. He felt like throwing up anyway, and his heart raced. The stiff slope of his shoulders became so heavy he was almost brought to his knees.

Patrick found what Wayne was stammering about in the spyglass, though he was not nearly as interested. He didn't know Annie and didn't think that anyone being in the crow's nest was something to get so excited about. He found Wayne's obsession, now reawakened, more tiresome than before. So much time had passed. There was nothing left to the story.

"We need to go there," Wayne said. "Something is happening."

"No, we don't," Patrick said. "Nothing good happens there."

"They're working together, I know it."

"So you've said."

"We have to stop them."

"No, we don't."

"They did this to you too," Wayne said. He was frustrated.

The fog was coming in so quickly that the crow's nest was already nearly out of view. Their fishing boat bobbed a little more roughly.

"What is it you think they're doing?" Patrick said. He was exhausted.

"I don't know. That's why we have to go there."

Wayne grabbed an oar and plunged it into the water with a dramatic, dragging sweep. The boat lurched and Patrick scrambled to get the net back inside. When they pulled onto the beach with an abrupt scrape, Wayne stalked off into the shadows toward Madam Toy's ship, but Patrick did not follow. Instead, he dragged the fishing boat back into the water and got inside. By the time Wayne reached the ship, the fog would conceal the crow's nest completely.

The main cabin of Madam Toy's *Fortune Lookie* was full—full glasses, full pockets, and full, bouncing bosoms. Madam Toy lounged in her chintz armchair while the girls paraded across the stage holding Chinese fans opened to hide their bodies, giving strategic glimpses of legs or bare shoulders or perhaps even panties.

Paloma made her way through the crowded room, collecting glasses from tables and generally hating life. Then she went to the kitchen to get the next basket of food for Juniper. Dolores had already prepared it; it sat on the countertop waiting for her.

"What's with this girl in the crow's nest?" Paloma asked Dolores.

"Well," Dolores said. She delighted in the chance to gossip. "I heard the Madam say the girl is cursed."

Paloma was not surprised when this came out of Dolores's mouth. Dolores was a big fan of curses. Paloma stared at her, blank and unbelieving.

"She's being saved," Dolores continued. "Very expensive. I saw Mei here."

"Who is that?"

"She is a snake." Dolores winked—an unsettling sight—and tapped the basket of food with her wooden spoon. Then she turned and carried on with her prayers.

Paloma took the basket outside to the deck, feeling suddenly hopeful that yet another untouched basket might come down. The fog kept the crow's nest from sight and dampened the glow of the lighthouse. She untied the ropes and moved the tray up.

The creak of the pulley startled Juniper. She was still horribly stuck to the topmast by her hair. Her head was snared so close to the pole that she'd become resigned to resting her face against it; no matter which way she turned, strands of hair pulled at her scalp like pinpricks. She would never be able to comb herself free.

The basket of food emerged through the fog and came to a stop. It swayed slightly.

"Help," Juniper said. She hadn't spoken a word in days. Her voice sounded strange. She felt too loud but knew she wasn't loud enough. There was no response. "Help!" she shouted, her throat cracking its way up in volume.

Paloma heard both of Juniper's pleas for help but, remembering that she'd already been scolded for talking to her, kept quiet. She shook the ropes to slap them against the pole, trying to speed up the process.

"Help!" Juniper shouted again, this time stretching the word wide and desperate.

When no response came, Juniper reached as far as she could and knocked the basket off the tray. It tumbled down, opening in the air as it fell, and rice, wet with gravy, emerged through the fog too fast for Paloma to move out of the way. The basket smacked her head and knocked her to the ground, where she found herself lying amid a great deal of Juniper's shed hair. The rice slid down Paloma's face, neck, and shoulders; the basket landed near her feet. With the immediate, savage anger that comes from something hitting you in the face, she yelled, "What the fuck!"—so loud that Juniper could hear her distinctly—and yanked on the ropes to bring the tray down as quickly as she could.

Then, confident that this was somehow the right move, Paloma scooted herself onto the tray, legs crossed and tucked beneath her. She started to pull herself up. The angle was uncomfortable and she was heavy. Her shoulders burned, and her forehead and temples became damp with sweat that cooled in the increasing wind, but she continued to drag herself higher into the air. Who the fuck was this girl up in the crow's nest, hidden like a pearl in an oyster, being so expensive? The strained spools whined at the top of the mast; the ropes frayed. Paloma was nearly to the crow's nest. She never paused to think what her next move would be, for this was an incomplete plan. All at once, Juniper and Paloma were eye to eye.

"What the fuck!" Paloma repeated, shouting just as loudly as she had from the deck.

Juniper didn't respond. There's seldom a convincing way to respond to someone saying that to you, especially a complete stranger, especially when your face is pushed up against a pole because your hair is tangled around and around it.

"What the fuck?" Paloma said. Her mind was not moving fast enough to come up with anything else to say. This time, however, her voice was soft and questioning. Of all the things she'd imagined the mysterious crow's nest girl to be, this wasn't it. This was pitiful. She'd expected some kind of snobby Oriental princess, but Juniper was just a little woodland animal caught in a bramble.

"Please help me," Juniper said. She held the comb out to Paloma as far as she could, but her reach was twisted and awkward from being stuck.

Paloma stepped into the crow's nest. She looked into the fog, seeing nothing but a faint orange glow from the lighthouse. It was unnerving, all that fog and no depth, alongside the unmistakable feeling of being very high up. She took the comb from Juniper. There was nothing to do but start untangling her hair.

"Thank you," Juniper whispered, the relief like a crashing wave.

Juniper was only comfortable if she kept her head bowed, eyes to the floor, where she could see Paloma's feet mixed up in her hair. Since they could not look at one another, they did not talk. Juniper missed her parents and she missed Mei. She held on to the mast with both arms to keep her weight from her neck. She listened to the flicking sounds of comb teeth on knots.

Paloma concentrated on getting the comb through the knots without hurting Juniper, but she couldn't tell root from end. There was just so much hair—longer than the crow's nest was tall, she was sure. It was inky black and shone almost blue under the dim lighthouse fire, and it gave Juniper the appearance of a fallen angel, its part like a spine between uncontainable wings. Paloma thought of her younger sisters. After their mother died, she had been in charge of the house. Their father was either gone or drunk, so she did all of the things a mother does. She did the cooking and cleaning, but she also loved. She comforted and combed hair, and she bore the sadness that comes with caring for a helpless thing that doesn't belong to you. And then leaving it.

Paloma worked on untangling Juniper, missing a time when she knew how to love, and Juniper worked on staying as comfortable as she could, missing a time when she felt loved. They each let their private homesickness envelop them until they intersected.

"Hey," Paloma said, breaking the silence. "Have you heard the story about the girl who ate an apple given to her by a snake and fell into a deep, deep sleep? The only thing that would wake her was a kiss from a prince—with tongue—but girls in long, deep sleep have pretty terrible breath, so it was too tall an order."

"No," Juniper said, meaning she hadn't heard that one.

"That was it," Paloma said. She wasn't sure Juniper understood. "The end," she added like an exclamation point.

Juniper exhaled a half laugh. This was an odd way to tell a story.

"What's your name?"

"Juniper."

"I'm Paloma."

Paloma managed to untangle enough of Juniper's hair for both of them to sit and face one another. Paloma saw that Juniper was very pretty, and also very afraid, though her fear was dampened to a flat, way-of-life type of fear. The sight of Juniper's caved frame and dim eyes escalated Paloma's sadness of a girl becoming a mother becoming a castoff, but the sadness was changing. Paloma felt destined for optimism, a feeling she'd nearly lost altogether after coming to the Barbary Coast. How graciously starvation turns itself hopeful again.

"How about another one? There was once a girl who hated peas, so when she was served mashed potatoes, she picked them out and hid them underneath her mattress. She slept just fine, because the peas had been boiled and there were no creeps watching her sleep. The end."

"Peas?"

"You're right, not a very good one," Paloma said. She freed another small section of Juniper's hair from the mast. Juniper felt a wave of relief at the back of her scalp.

"There was once a girl who wore a red kerchief when she went walking through the forest. She was selling bibles door to door and nobody likes that, so a wolf ate her. The end."

"What's a bible?"

Paloma found herself speechless. She blew right past it. "There was once a fair maiden who fell in love with a toad, which was just fine, for men are assholes and toads do make lovely pets. The end."

Juniper was getting sleepy. The feel of Paloma, her body so close, her hands kind and gentle, made her the most relaxed she'd felt in a long time. She allowed the stories, as strange as they were, to lull her, concentrating on the cadence of a storyteller's speech.

"There was once a mermaid who wanted to be human so badly that she let a sea witch cut out her tongue in exchange for a fine pair of lady legs. But the man she loved wasn't much interested in a girl with no tongue, so while he was sleeping she cut his tongue out too. He still left her. And the poor lady mermaid was stuck being a lonely, mute human girl. The end."

* * *

Paloma slid her fingers through Juniper's hair between brush strokes. When she grazed Juniper's neck or shoulders or back with her fingertips, Juniper shivered, her shoulders briefly lifting, her skin dotting with little bumps.

Juniper's breath slowed and joined the current of Paloma's hands moving through her hair. Her body was a part of the tide, rocking in the waves, and she let herself doze.

III

The Lighthouse Keeper shifts in her chair. She shoves the blanket from her lap abruptly, then feels the chill and petulantly pulls it back over her legs. She's fussy, agitated. You haven't yet seen her make such sharp movements, and you feel insecure. You feel responsible for her feelings, whatever they are. But the only thing worse than being responsible for her being upset is to continue compounding it, so, as has been your way since entering the lighthouse, you pretend not to exist.

Instead, you think about laundry and how vastly you've underestimated its inconvenience. You think about the intimacy of another person's hands in your hair. You think about how the fire has grown low again and feel nervous watching it. You are pulled from your thoughts when the Lighthouse Keeper shifts in her chair again. She picks up her teacup but finds it empty. This annoys her, but she doesn't move to make more. You feel guilty that your cup is still half full, like its plenty mocks her. You hesitate, wondering if you should drink it down quickly, stuck

between the fear of appearing wasteful and the fear of appearing
snide. But she's not paying attention to you or your teacup. You
don't exist; only the rest of the story does.

Wayne stayed in the shadows of the cliffside when he reached Madam Toy's *Fortune Lookie*. He was close enough to see but too far away to hear, and the heavy fog was making the seeing part increasingly difficult. He'd watched this ship so many times on so many nights. Nothing looked particularly different now; he knew it was different, he just couldn't see it. He had seen someone in the crow's nest who was now hidden in the fog. He also saw what he always saw—a steady trickle of solitary men who came to Madam Toy's doorstep and disappeared inside. Wayne knew that inside was where the answers were and, for the first time since losing that fateful hand of poker, he would go there.

Wayne slunk closer to the ship. He was excited, fervently so. His mind raced with the vague idea that justice was about to be served. This was Wayne Jimbo's chance, dammit. But he had no idea what was going to happen between this moment in the shadows and the moment he would walk away a vindicated hero.

The ship was as strange to him as it had been the first and only time he'd stepped aboard. Since then he'd only observed the ship like a caricature in the newspaper, demonizing her, warping her into new, more horrible creations. Madam Toy and her ship and her conspirators and her serpentine business were mythical, and Wayne was ready to reenter the story. He was ready to fuck shit up.

He managed to slip inside and take a seat in a corner behind a large man without drawing any attention to himself. He scanned the room and saw Madam Toy seated at a table by herself, counting coins and shoving them between her tits, which were pushed up to her chin. Madam Toy did not look like she'd aged at all. She looked as beautiful and commanding as she had fifteen years ago, perhaps more so.

One of Madam Toy's girls was dancing on stage, fluttering a large cloth fan to give peeks of her mostly naked body. Another half dozen girls were weaving among the tables of drinking men, perching on the armrests of their chairs, bathing them with the scent of sugary perfume, and taking flirtatious sips from their tumblers of whiskey. The room was oddly quiet for one so crowded. The girls did not know any English, and men don't talk much with other men in such a situation. There was wordless music, the muffled whooshing of fans, the clink of glasses on tables, the inhibited sighs of nearly pleased men; the rest was the silence of dreamy enrapture.

A girl came and stood behind Wayne. She ran her hands over his shoulders and down his chest, then brought her face down right beside his ear and ever so faintly moaned. He felt her hair on the back of his neck. He felt her breath, her skin, her heat. She came to sit on the arm of his chair. He put his hands on her, but she moved them away coyly. She put her hands on herself, moving them up and down her thighs, over her breasts, tracing her fingertips on her throat; Wayne watched and imagined that his hands were her hands and her hands were in his pants. He considered giving up on his mission and paying Madam Toy to take this girl downstairs. He patted his pocket to hear the click of coins, then glanced around the large man who hid him from Madam Toy's view, where he found Madam Toy waiting for his eyes to meet hers, as if that faint sound of coins had alerted her to the presence of prey. She was tensed to spring; he could see it in the tilt of her chin and the perfect stillness of her neck and shoulders.

The girl on the arm of his chair continued to press her body against him. She ran her hands over the base of his neck and then up into his hair. Her skin smelled like sunlight, even inside the darkened room under the foggy night sky. But he couldn't see her anymore, for nothing else existed besides Madam Toy's transfixed eyes and the smile that held in its corners Wayne's buckling pride and all the smallness that could be drawn from a bruised man. And he couldn't feel the girl beside him anymore. He only felt how stupid it was to think he could ever be anything but what he was.

Madam Toy was coming over to him, her walk slow and sinful, and Wayne would always remember how bizarre it was to watch her approach while the girl at his side, who didn't belong in this moment, touched him. His heartbeat was too fast. His ears were fuzzy like the sound of tall grass in a breeze. His mind was dauntingly blank. He remembered how he had gotten there but not why, or perhaps it was the other way around. He'd wanted to look Madam Toy dead in the eye and know that she knew, finally, that she'd never had him fooled. But that was not how Madam Toy was looking at him, and he found he could barely endure her gaze for even a few seconds. He'd imagined this moment so many times without imagining it at all, preparing for the end with no beginning.

"You've come back to see your auntie," Madam Toy said. She had an eerie sweetness in her voice. The girl who sat on the arm of Wayne's chair stood to leave, but Madam Toy stopped her. "Is this what you've come for?" she said, gesturing to the girl. "You have good taste." The girl softened at Madam Toy's compliment.

Wayne shifted in his seat, feeling just as young and poor and desperate as he had fifteen years ago. What was it he had wanted to say? Madam Toy was in front of him, so close, and he had spent fifteen years blaming her for his lot in life; he remembered her wickedness and her voice and her breasts full of other people's dignity. But she was not like his memory, and he was not like his fantasy, and none of this was at all what he'd hoped for. All the things he could never say were built into a lump in his throat that he tried to swallow down so it would unravel and disperse and he might just say something, anything at all. But he couldn't. The bubble of obsession he'd created, now punctured, left among its broken pieces a deep embarrassment.

"I suppose I can't blame you," Madam Toy said. "I took a girl from you, and now you want one in return."

Wayne looked up at the girl and admired her smooth skin and expression of ease, of not knowing and not knowing there was anything to know. He thought back to the night fifteen years ago at the poker table and then to this night when, even after everything in between, nothing had changed at all.

"The girl," Madam Toy said. But instead of pointing to Annie, she pointed to this one, and instead of demand there was expectation, and instead of the possibility he felt with a hand of cards there was surrender and a few coins in his pocket.

When he handed the money over, he felt the relief of

doing what Madam Toy wanted. The girl's hand was a buoy; her body was the tide moving onto shore, and she was easy to follow downstairs into a dim room.

When Paloma had finished combing out Juniper's hair, she braided it while Juniper continued to doze. She thought about her old life, her sisters, the orange groves. She thought about her new life, about wanting to leave and having no way to do it. She thought that Juniper might be the answer; she'd never had a friend before. They could leave together, get away from Madam Toy and this place. With each turn of the braid, she felt like she was pulling herself closer to her dream, and her resolve hardened.

"We should leave," Paloma said as soon as she finished braiding.

Juniper blinked away her nap. She looked toward the lighthouse. She couldn't see the structure through the fog, but she saw the smear of orange firelight it created. Mei hadn't come for her; there was no sign she would.

"And go where?" Juniper said.

"I don't know," Paloma said. "Does it matter? You don't want to stay here, trust me."

Juniper felt exposed. Her thoughts turned inward, reconsidering what she thought about the things she didn't know, suspecting that Paloma did know them and feeling like maybe not knowing was easier. She couldn't bring herself to say anything.

"You should think about it," Paloma said, sensing she wasn't going to get her answer so soon. She smiled at Juniper, realizing how foreign a smile felt. She slid back onto the pulley tray and lowered herself back down through the fog. She would have to find out what Dolores knew; then she and Juniper could leave. The end.

Lowering herself was not as easy as Paloma expected. She was so heavy that she had to cling to the rope to keep from freely plummeting. Her hands burned. She forced herself not to look down, but she had spent so much time hanging laundry on the riggings that she knew she was still high in the air. She sweated with the strain and fear. She was having a hard time keeping her grip on the rope. She wasn't going fast enough to make it to the ground before she couldn't hold on any longer. She tried to hurry, but it made her hands slip and burn even worse than before.

She let herself drop from a ways above the deck and crashed down with a loud thud. She landed in the wet, ricey mess of Juniper's wasted dinner. She panted, stood, and brushed the food from her clothes.

Madam Toy heard the noise on the deck. She went outside, where she found Paloma, her clothes covered in food. She immediately panicked, knowing from Paloma's sweaty, flushed face that she had done something to make contact with Juniper. She looked back over her shoulder to make sure she hadn't been followed.

"I told you to stay away from her," Madam Toy spat.

"Who is she?" Paloma spat back, fatigued and suddenly angry.

"Look who's interested in how I make my money," Madam Toy said. Her demeanor had shifted. She spoke softly, threateningly, and very close to Paloma's face. "You don't belong here," Madam Toy continued. "And now you've gone and made yourself a problem. What do you think should happen to girls that make problems?"

Paloma didn't say anything in return. She felt her newfound hope leave her like a carriage full of oranges disappearing down the road. She could hear the wheels rolling away, see the tracks they left in the dust, feel the ache of understanding. She looked up but couldn't see the crow's nest through the fog. How quickly hope turns to nothing at all. There was only going back inside to the kitchen.

The lighthouse fire had been lit for a few hours now, and Mei hadn't moved since lighting it. She stood back from the window so her shadow could not be seen and watched. She watched the fog come in. She heard the murmurs of voices on the air, one of which she knew was Juniper's. She waited for something without knowing what. She wanted to see, felt frustrated with her own hesitation, and blamed the fog. She should be over there, taking her place beside Madam Toy for the last time. Then maybe she would be able to forget. Or maybe she would die and become nothing, and wouldn't that be everything?

Uneven gusts of wind came suddenly off the Pacific, and the lighthouse fire sputtered. The fog shifted, thin streams moving west like water. Mei couldn't tell if the fog was moving forward or if she was moving backward. Her body swayed in the confusion, her head light, until the world stabilized again. When it did, the wind, for just a second, made a pocket of clear air around Madam Toy's ship. The red lanterns were aglow. There was the vibrating hum of a crowd. There was the crow's nest and Juniper inside. There was the deck; coming aboard was Mr. Zhou, and there to receive him was Madam Toy.

Mei was moving back in time.

The sky was the same sky. The stars were the same stars. Mei was looking at Juniper but she was seeing herself. She was seeing the way her story began: *There was a girl whose life was promised to a man who came by ship to take her away.* She and Juniper were the same—the innocence in the flushed cheeks, the body straight and slender, the vulnerability of the untamed. Young. But they were not the same. Something was missing in Juniper, something that Mei had had—a recklessness that comes when one's vulnerability is realized. It was the difference between them. Mei had fought back; she had run away, because she had at least known that she could. The scene unfolding before her eyes was her story, but it wasn't. She finally saw that she'd made it Juniper's, too; for this, she felt sorry.

Suddenly Mei felt she was being carried farther and farther out to sea with no way back. She was too full of tears that wouldn't fall, screams that wouldn't sound, fires that would burn out long before she could consider forgiveness. Time was stuck but soon enough would continue rushing past, and for the first time, Mei was desperate for the current. How dare time stop in this moment. How dare the ship, the man, the trade. How dare she.

Mei was having a hard time breathing. A fate is made of water, made to fit itself into the last spaces left open in a life. But what happens when the only space left will take away the air? The tension of the moment weighed her down. The pocket of clear sky around the ship was losing its contours; new fog drifted into its place. Mr. Zhou and Madam Toy slipped behind the veil of it. The ship's lanterns were obscured to a vague flush. For one heart-stopping second, there was only Juniper, high in the crow's nest, alone and floating.

Mei stood beside the fire, hoping that if she didn't move, the world might forget she had ever been a part of it. She would not go down to the ship. She would let Mr. Zhou wait there in vain and leave empty-handed, his fee unpaid and without the girl. She would abandon Juniper to whatever life she could make for herself, though Mei knew exactly what she'd left her to: Madam Toy would claim her. Was that better than being an orphan? She couldn't say.

Then, with a last gust of wind, the scene was gone, hidden again behind the depthless fog. Mei was surrounded by an amount of gold as dense and deep as need, as soft as a desperate woman's conviction—and she was so sorry. *Once upon a very long time ago, in a country where the river runs over a bed of pearls . . . here in this lighthouse she is cursed.* Here is where Mei, the maker of Gold Mountain, will remain.

You can tell the Lighthouse Keeper is done with her story by the way her voice has become so throttled. You have never experienced a silence as empty as this one. You aren't ready for the story to be over; the ending came too fast and doesn't feel enough like an ending for you to accept. You're frustrated.

"Is that the end?" you ask, because you feel the need to make sure. Your voice scrapes in your throat and sounds strange to you.

"I suppose it depends. Is it what you were looking for?" she says.

You aren't sure. How could you be sure? If you don't know what comes next, you can't discern whether or not you were looking for whatever it is.

"What happened next?" you ask.

"At first, not much. When Mei did not come for her, Juniper became another of Madam Toy's girls. She didn't have much choice. Then, she got pregnant." She's more matter-of-fact now.

There's a liveliness in her voice that hints she is just about ready for you to leave.

But you're not going to leave yet, because yes, you were looking for this. If Juniper had a baby, the story, almost a perfect replica of the one before, might start over—another ring in the rippling water, another opportunity for Mei to break her curse, even though you know she never did; she's still here in her lighthouse, after all. And anyway, your question was never about her curse. You try to make it obvious that you're waiting for more without asking, and you can see she understands.

"She had a son," the Lighthouse Keeper says. "And she died giving birth," she adds, almost whispering. As soon as you hear it, you know that this is what she was avoiding. You try to change the subject.

"What happened to Wayne? And Paloma?" you ask.

"I don't know," she says. "They lived, they died. Same as what happens to everyone else." She says it in a way that's meant to shut you down.

"What happened before 1849?" you try.

"I was lonely. There were natives, then missionaries, but I kept my distance. I collected in secret, careful not to expose what was hidden. I did this," she said, gesturing to the room around her and all its gold. You see her relief at talking about something else, but you decide to renege on the change of subject.

"The Gold Rush is why all this happened?" you say, somewhere between a question and a statement.

She doesn't answer. A faraway look comes into her eyes.

"Right?" you ask. "Because if the gold hadn't been found, then…" You trail off, hoping she will pick up and finish the rest of the sentence. She doesn't.

Really, though, you don't need her to answer, because you know. If the gold hadn't been discovered, the Gold Rush would never have begun. There wouldn't have been the Barbary Coast or its people or its schemes. Mei might have gotten all the gold back and wouldn't have had to hand over a virgin to break her curse. She wouldn't have done to Juniper exactly what she'd run away from. But even though you know this, you want her to say it. You aren't sure why, but you feel the need to challenge her; you can't help yourself.

"What happened next?" you ask, by which you mean to ask what happened to the baby. You insert a little entitlement into your tone, hoping it will get you answers, but the wistful expression leaves her face. Her shoulders rise. Her face is drawn with skepticism.

"Why did you come here?" she asks.

You aren't sure what to say. You came with a ready answer for this question, but you don't feel like explaining the orphan in your bloodline. It doesn't really matter. What matters is the story. It was always about the story.

You feel ready to leave now. Even the embers of the fire are almost out; the cold has come back in sneaking wisps. You shift to stand up, put your hands on your knees, and realize you haven't moved in a long time. You're stiff and slow, but you think feeling this way is somehow inappropriate for the moment. You push yourself to your feet with a great effort not to voice the struggle. You let her question go stale in the air without an answer.

"Thank you, A-Yi," you say, and you make for the door—feeling just for a second the pain that comes with leaving a child or an elder alone in the night.

About the Author

Caitlin Chung has lived in the Bay Area her whole life. She is a teacher, an expert eavesdropper, and a fan of infomercials, and is known to be a supporter of superstitions. She has on many occasions been justly accused of being a Luddite. She lives in Oakland with her husband and their cat. This is her first book.

Acknowledgements

Kilby—I would be lost without you, most likely somewhere in a parking lot. Happy random day of every month forever.

Charlie Kennedy—you always remind me of the work it takes to write, and that I can do it.

The Oak Street Apartment Poets:
Tony Degenaro—you have the biggest heart I've ever known.
Calvin Fantone, and also Kevin—you saved me from the couch.

Oakland—my home.

Kate Malmgren—my person-home.

TJ DiFrancesco—I wanted to be cool like you, so I started writing.

My CC Family, especially Amy Crudo, Leslie Crosby, and Katie Murphy—how do you have all the wisdom?

To all my students—your strange little minds give me life. I facetiously told you I'd include you in the acknowledgments, but you didn't know what facetiously means, so here we are.

Odie—you might just be a cat, but I think that you would know if I didn't thank you, and that you would be very unforgiving about it.

Lanternfish Press—Christine Neulieb, Feliza Casano, Amanda Thomas, Aubry Norman—thank you for choosing me. It's been a great adventure and I am forever grateful.